OUTLAWS:

Six Guns

*Also by Chet Cunningham
in Large Print:*

Battle Cry
Fort Blood
Renegade Army
Sioux Showdown

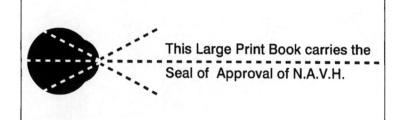

OUTLAWS:

Six Guns

CHET CUNNINGHAM

Thorndike Press • Waterville, Maine

Copyright © 1989 by Chet Cunningham/BookCrafters
Book 2 in the Outlaws Series.

Published in 2002 by arrangement with Chet Cunningham.

Thorndike Press Large Print Western Series.

The tree indicium is a trademark of Thorndike Press.

The text of this Large Print edition is unabridged.
Other aspects of the book may vary from the original edition.

Set in 16 pt. Plantin.

Printed in the United States on permanent paper.

Library of Congress Cataloging-in-Publication Data

Cunningham, Chet.
  Six guns / Chet Cunningham.
    p. cm. — (Outlaws ; 2)
  ISBN 0-7862-4467-4 (lg. print : hc : alk. paper)
  1. Comanche Indians — Fiction. 2. Massacres — Fiction.
3. Outlaws — Fiction. 4. Revenge — Fiction. 5. Wyoming
— Fiction. 6. Large type books. I. Title.
PS3553.U468 S59 2002
  813′.54—dc21   2002028565

OUTLAWS:

Six Guns

CHAPTER

ONE

Rock Springs, Wyoming: August 14, 1869

The Professor looked at the five men sitting around the table at the Wild Card saloon in Rock Springs and laughed softly, his clean-shaven face serious for the moment.

The man was dressed immaculately in black suit, red, white, and silver fancy vest with gold watch, chain and fob, and a set of spit-polished, 50-dollar cowboy boots.

"Gentlemen, we can do it," the Professor said softly. The men had to lean to hear him over the chatter and clatter of the saloon. "This is the perfect spot. Rock Springs has been here for maybe two years. It was one of the towns the railroad had to spot along the tracks every fifty miles. Isn't this about the widest-open town we've been in for a long time?"

The Professor looked around at the other men at the table. Eagle, a full-blooded Comanche Indian, had cut his long hair and wore standard cowboy clothes and hat in an attempt to pass as white. It usually worked. He shrugged at the question.

Johnny Joe Williams worked a deck of cards in a riffle shuffle and began another hand of blackjack with himself. Johnny Joe was about five-eight, lean, with a plain buckskin vest.

"Safe bet with me either way," he said.

Juan Romero shook his head. "I don't see how we can do it. Even if we wear masks they will remember our size and how we were dressed."

Gunner Johnson, at six-four the biggest man in the group, saw the Professor look at him and shrugged. Gunner was tall and broad, made of solid muscle, but he was not a mental giant.

Willy Boy, the sixth man at the table, had been grinning since the idea came forth.

"Hell yes, let's try it," he said. "For me it would be a real kick in the ass to rob the damned bank and walk around town calm as you please watching these jackasses try to figure out who did it and which way they rode out of town!"

The Professor nodded and sat down at

the table. "So, this is the last time we are seen together in public. Meet tonight at my room at seven o'clock and we'll plan it out." He looked at Willy Boy.

"Sounds fine by me," Willy Boy said. "Now let's scatter; two's is fine, but no more. Today is Thursday." He looked at the Professor. "You want to do a Friday afternoon kind of relief job on the bank?" He spoke in a low voice, the last line almost a whisper.

The Professor grinned. "Don't know yet. I'll go get some change this afternoon and figure it out. Either way it's gonna be as easy as skinning a fancy lady out of her underwear on a Saturday night."

Four of the men nodded and left the table. One stayed at the bar for another beer. Willy Boy and Gunner Johnson stayed at the table.

"It'll be all right, Gunner. The Professor knows what he's doing. We'll come out in fine shape. Had to let the boys blow off a little steam. Hell, we're still a long ways from Boise and Idaho Territory. Our cash reserves are getting a mite low anyway, and we got nobody on our trail."

"Yeah, I understand, Willy Boy. Whatever you want is fine with me."

"Good, Gunner, good. I can always

count on you. Why don't you go over to the bar and get us a couple more of them cold beers?" He gave Gunner a dime. The big man heaved up from the chair, almost knocking it over, and strode to the bar. Soon he came back with two more beers.

"Gunner, this is going to be wild, absolutely crazy good!" Willy Boy said in a voice so low Gunner had to lean close to hear it. "I ain't never even heard of a gang robbing a bank and staying right in the same town. It's wild, crazy, and just might work. If it don't work, the Professor will have us do it the regular way and we'll be out of town heading west before anybody knows the bank has been busted."

They sipped at their beers.

Willy Boy was the leader of the Willy Boy Gang. They had formed when he fooled a jailer in Oak Park, Texas into opening his jail cell. He'd overpowered the man and shot him in the head. Willy Boy and the other five prisoners in the little jail escaped and formed a group to battle off the posse that chased after them. They shot up the posse twice and the sheriff gave up.

A week later, the famous bounty hunter Michael Handshoe and his own gang of shooters pursued them. After three furious gun battles, Handshoe admitted he was beaten and rode away. He wasn't used to going up against an organized gang of men who knew how to shoot.

The Willy Boy Gang worked together like a well-oiled machine. Each man had a special role. They had come up this far on their way to Boise, in Idaho Territory. By now there also were wanted posters out on them with a value of $2,000 each. It was an attractive package for any man to try to collect. Since most cowhands worked for $25 a month and store clerks took in about $35 a month, $12,000 for the six of them was a fortune — more than 28 years' pay at $420 a year. They had to keep up their guard all the time.

Boise. The long trip to Idaho was for Eagle. He was tracking down Able troop of the Fourteenth Cavalry Regiment. The regiment had been assigned to Boise to help on the Indian wars.

Eagle wasn't a big talker. He did say that six years ago the Fourteenth had been stationed in Texas and Able company had been sent out to try to move a small band of Comanche into a reservation. The band, not more than 25 warriors, women, and children, had given up and were getting ready to take down their camp and move

11

with the soldiers.

Someone started shooting, and before anyone could stop it, the 45 troopers and officers had killed everyone in the camp, except for one 12-year-old boy. Eagle was then known as Brave Eagle. After his best friend had been killed, he was captured by Able company and its violence-prone leader, Captain Two-Guns Riley. Eagle was sent to a Catholic boarding school, where he was taught to read and write English.

Now he was a man of 18. He lived to find Able company and pay back in blood for the blood of his family and friends spilled that fateful day in Texas.

Willy Boy pushed back from the table. "Gunner, looks like it's near to supper time. How about you and me heading over to that little tent café we saw this morning?"

They met at seven that evening in the Professor's room at the Rock Springs Hotel. It was one of about 20 frame buildings in town. There were still 20 or 30 tents set up as businesses and homes. Lumber cost a lot of money. In time the tents would be replaced with frame buildings.

The Professor was the best dresser of the

group. He was also the oldest at 25. Willy Boy was still surprised that the man had gone through high school and had taken a whole year of college! He then taught school for two years before heading west.

The Professor pushed his polished boot up on a chair and grinned. "Gentlemen, the Rock Springs Home Bank is made out of cardboard and cotton. It will be the easiest that I have ever attempted to relieve of its burden of cash.

"This afternoon I visited the establishment. It has one teller, one bookkeeper, and an owner-president. Three men. Easy!

"There is one door at the front and another leading to the alley.

"I suggest we do our Friday-at-quitting-time ritual on these men, but add one wrinkle — we blindfold them as soon as we get them under control so they have less time to look at us.

"You know the procedure. We all drop in to the bank three minutes before closing time with 'business' to transact. We help lock the door and pull the blinds. We tie, gag, and blindfold the three of them and any customers. Then we clean out the teller's till and the vault. We leave the bankers and customers well tied and out of sight, and slip out the back door, with

13

greenbacks and gold sticking out of our pockets.

"I don't expect a big strike here, but it will be worthwhile, with the railroad business and the gambling halls. Any questions?"

"We wear neckerchief masks like before?" Eagle asked.

"Right. As soon as the door is locked, we pull up the masks, tie up the men, then gag and blindfold them."

"We come back here to leave the money after the robbery?" Willy Boy asked. "Then at least nobody could catch us with it on us."

"Yes, good idea, Willy Boy. We'll do that. If we take any bank bags, we have to keep them under our coats. Let's not wear our long coats this time. Too damn hot for them, and it would give us away. No shotguns. We won't need them. I'll find two or three paper or cloth sacks we can use to carry the loot in."

"Horses?" Johnny Joe asked.

The Professor looked at Willy Boy.

"We shouldn't need them," Willy Boy said quickly. "But I've lived long enough to know that sometimes simple jobs like this can go wrong. We better be packed up for the trail, with the horses left along the street nearest the bank alley. We don't want to get caught with no way to get out of town if we have to leave sudden-like."

The Professor looked at the men again. There were no more questions.

"Guess that about does it," Willy Boy said. "I don't want anybody getting passing-out, soused drunk tonight or wind up in jail. We have to be clear-eyed and ready for business tomorrow at 2:30."

They split up.

Johnny Joe Williams went to the best gambling hall in town. It was a tent half a block from the tracks and had been there for over two years, set up when the tracks were about 20 miles east of the newly established town.

Johnny Joe was the gambler in the group. He had been a lawman for a year when he was charged with murder while performing his duty. He had quietly left town one night, and then traveled half the west, spending a year on the Mississippi River gambling boats.

Johnny Joe was the son of a Southern plantation owner who lost everything in the war, including his own life and the lives of most of his family. Johnny Joe was 17 when the war ended, living in New Orleans with an aunt. She had taught him how to play poker. She was an expert who had dealt cards for a while in a gambling hall. He had decided not to go back and try to claim the old homestead. Things were a lot different right after the war.

Poker was his game. He never bet unless he knew he had a good chance of winning. He played the game by the odds and by his head, and almost always won more than he lost.

Eagle went for a long walk into the prairie, looked for shooting stars, listened to the nighthawks, and watched the small night-feeding animals, who didn't realize he was there. He loved to sit alone out there at night and get back to the essentials of life — wind, sky, the land, nature itself.

The Professor went back to the Prairie West Saloon and lost five dollars at poker. Then he took one of the dance hall girls upstairs for a serious conversation and to investigate her inner self.

Juan Romero was not welcome at most of the saloons and at none of the gambling halls. He bought a pint bottle of wine and went back to his room, where he wrote a long letter to his wife. He mailed it to his uncle in Oak Park, Texas who would forward it to Juan's wife in Mexico, or take it to her.

Gunner Johnson followed Willy Boy to the Blue Bottom Saloon and watched him play dime-limit poker. Willy Boy lost four dollars in four hours. They listened to a faded dove singing to an out-of-tune piano, then after three beers went back to the hotel and bed.

Willy Boy Lambier was the leader of the gang both by design and default. He had pretended to hang himself in that jail cell back in Texas, then shot the deputy with his own gun when the foolish lawman charged into the cell to rescue Willy Boy.

He was waiting trial on a murder charge and was sure to be convicted and hung. He had nothing to lose. Neither did three of the other men in the jail. Willy Boy forced them all to make the break with him. He convinced them they could stay free only if they bound themselves together in a gang to fight off the posse that would surely follow.

The ploy had worked. They had stayed together, partly from loyalty, partly from fear, but mostly because each of them had a dream or a cause or revenge to carry out, and the gang was the best way to help them accomplish it.

Willy Boy had a shot at avenging his father. Willy Boy had been orphaned at 14, when a bounty hunter charged into his father's poor Missouri farmhouse and shotgunned him without a word. Only then did the bounty hunter realize he had the wrong man, so he tried to kill the only witness, too.

But Willy Boy broke out a window and fled screaming and bleeding into the night as shotgun and pistol roared behind him. Since that day he had been living only to find the murdering bounty hunter, Deeds Conover, and torture him until he died.

Willy Boy had grown up fast. He made his living by rolling drunks in saloons, picking their pockets as he helped them stagger to the outhouse.

He was attacked by a man in Kansas City, had his horse and all his gear stolen. He was caught trying to pick another drunk's pocket, and killed a man before he was finally captured and jailed. Soon after, he killed the guard and broke out of jail, heading for Texas, where Deeds Conover had gone.

Willy Boy was 17 now, with more than a dozen notches on his gun, a growing hatred in his heart, and a surprising sense of loyalty to his gang. He still wanted Conover. He had two shots at killing him in Kansas but missed. Now it was Eagle's turn to find the men who had killed his family.

The wheel kept spinning. Willy Boy knew that sooner or later he would be face-to-face with Deeds Conover, and he damn well wouldn't let the bastard get away again.

Willy Boy turned it all over in his mind. He was surprised that he was going to all this trouble to help the Indian. He hardly knew the man, but now they were a team, a gang, a fighting unit that could handle almost any situation.

He grinned in the darkness of the Rocky Springs Hotel. Tomorrow they'd rob the crackerbox of a bank and loaf around town two or three days, watching the natives try to catch the robbers. Then they would move northwest toward Pocatello in Idaho on the way to Boise.

Willy Boy frowned for a minute. The other night around the campfire, Juan Romero had said he was getting a good feeling about their gang. He said that they trusted each other and worked together. He said it was almost the way he used to feel about his big family in Mexico.

Willy Boy thought about that. A family. He'd never had a family feeling at all. Just him and his pa as long as he could remember. Yeah, it was something good. Better than he had ever known before. Goddamn, they had themselves a family here!

Willy smiled softly and drifted off to sleep.

CHAPTER

TWO

Deputy Seth Andrews, of the Oak Park Sheriff's Department had waited a week before he left town to chase Willy Boy. He'd seen the tattered remains of the Sheriff's posse, and then seen Sheriff Dunwoody himself come straggling back alone after a second try to take Willy Boy with six more fighting men. Seth cried at the terrible loss of human life.

Seth Andrews had listened to everything the sheriff told him about the battles, the ambushes, how damn *good* those six bastards were with their weapons and their tactics. Seth had descriptions of and details about each of the six men in the gang written down in a small notebook he carried. He was determined to bring them back, dead or alive — he didn't care which way.

For three days he had pleaded with the Sheriff to keep him on the payroll and send him after the six men. Sheriff Dunwoody said he'd had enough good men killed. "Let them go, let them go to hell! Forget them." But Deputy Andrews couldn't let go of it. He had told the Sheriff he was going, took a six-month leave of absence from the department without pay, and set out to run down Willy Boy and his gang.

Seth had just turned 35. His head wasn't healed up yet, but Doc Farnam said to put the salve on it and change the bandage every three days. If he kept his hat on, nobody could tell he'd been head-shot.

Doc Farnam assured him that there had been no real damage, just a crease across his skull. He had bled like a stuck hog at butchering time. Of course, the blow on the head left him dazed and disoriented for a day or two. Doc Farnam said the powder burns were the worst part — scorched off a three-inch strip of his hair and burned his scalp black. The wound would heal in a few weeks, and his hair should even grow back in.

Deputy Andrews got to keep his badge and had the Sheriff sign a letter of authorization to apprehend the six men. He also had fifty wanted posters of the Willy Boy Gang stuffed into one of his saddlebags.

Seth was not married. He had wanted to

be a lawman since he was a small boy. He had finally made it here in Oak Park. There had been no training, no law instruction, nothing to teach him how to be a deputy sheriff. His only instruction was to do what the sheriff told him, and hope that he didn't get himself killed.

He had always been a good deputy. He had shown real concern about the welfare of the men he captured and jailed. If he hadn't been so concerned, (about Willy Boy when he obviously was dying by hanging) he would not have tried to save Willy Boy when he had tried to hang himself in his cell. And then, this whole tragedy wouldn't have happened.

Seth sat on his horse that Saturday morning and watched Sheriff Dunwoody.

"I be going now, Sheriff," Seth said.

"Reckon I can't stop you. You get back in a month, your job's still open. Longer than that, I got to hire me a new man, Seth. You know that for sure?"

"I understand that, Sheriff. This is just something I got to do. If it wasn't for what I done back there in the jail, fifteen good men wouldn't be dead right now. Got to make up for that, one way or another, or die trying."

He nodded, and then rode north. The

last contact with the Willy Boy Gang had been that bounty hunter in Dodge City, Kansas. Seth figured he'd start there. Tracking six men in a group shouldn't be all that hard. There would be violence and lawbreaking, no matter where they went. That would make it easier.

Seth Andrews slumped as he rode north. He was not a big man, five-seven and slender. But he was tough enough to be a deputy sheriff. He'd come up through the cowboy route, working cows and doing a trail drive or two. Then, when he was 23 he had a chance to become a deputy sheriff in Oak Park. He had been there ever since.

Until now.

His face was stretched wide, all angles and bones sticking out from clean-shaven cheeks. He had a hawk nose over a thin mouth that might look cruel on some faces, but not on Seth's. His eyes were deep set and wary, now and again showing traces of the pain that darted through his scalp, where the burned tissue was gamely working at restoring itself.

He rode north without complaint. He'd take the stage when he could. Maybe the train. He'd sell his horse and buy another when needed.

Seth set his broad, bony jaw. His face

was weathered from days in the sunshine and wind. His light brown eyes seemed to sink deeper into his skull each year. His brown hair was seared away now on the left side where the part should be. Another two weeks before his scalp would heal up, the doctor had said. Somehow Seth figured his hair never would grow in. He could take to wearing interesting little soft caps.

He was rawboned and thin. He wore sturdy denim pants and a tan shirt with a vest in brown leather. He had packed carefully. No newcomer to trail riding, he knew exactly what he needed and what he could do without. He brought two complete changes of clothes and six pairs of socks. He would buy new clothes as he needed them.

Seth had packed a small coffee pot and had ground his coffee before he left, so he didn't need to pack along a grinder. He had a canvas bag for his camping and food supplies. Nothing that would spoil quickly. Bacon was his only concession there, along with a loaf of home-baked bread. He'd eat in towns and stage stops whenever he could.

He hadn't gone to the ambush site. He didn't want to see it. It would only make him more angry. Seth had all the anger he could hold now. Those six men did not deserve to live. They had broken out of jail. They had killed at least 18 men, including posse members and lawmen. They should be hunted down and shot like rabid wolves.

Which was exactly what he intended to do.

He was well armed. Seth had a Spencer rifle and a Blakeslee Quickloader that held 13 tubes of ammunition to reload the Spencer repeating rifle.

His sidearm was a Colt, reworked to take solid .45 rounds. He had 200 rounds for each weapon.

He carried a poncho to turn the rain away and a rain hat, but no second pair of boots.

Seth made it to Dodge City after a week and a half. Sheriff Ralph Groller looked at his letter and snorted.

"Yeah, they were here, at least a bounty hunter by the handle of Michael Handshoe said they were. He come in here snorting fire, waving that wanted poster, and asking my help. He found them all right. First, here in town at the hotel. He tried to take them with ten men. He lost three men there. Then he chased them out of town a ways. Somebody reported the firing and we investigated. We found four more of Handshoe's men dead, and then Handshoe himself. The top of his head was blown off and the gun was still in his hand. Seems Handshoe got shot up real bad, dying slow, so he ended it all himself."

"All that gunplay and you didn't go after the gang?" Deputy Seth Andrews asked.

The Dodge City Sheriff moved to an easier position in his soft chair and shook his head. "Time we heard about it and got out there the Willy Boy Gang had faded into the plains, generally heading north and west. Not a lot we could do. Never have been real enthusiastic about these bounty hunters anyway. This bunch just met a crew they couldn't handle. Ain't like going up against one man on the run."

"Sheriff Groller, did you see any of the six in the gang? Did one of them check with you about another bounty hunter, Deeds Conover?"

"Matter of fact, one of them did. I didn't pay any attention at the time. Lots of bounty hunters try to keep track of other bounty hunters."

"Which one was it who checked with you?"

"As I recall, Handshoe told me it must

27

have been the tall one, the Professor. I can't remember rightly now. That was two, three weeks ago. Handshoe tried to take them in their rooms first. He captured one of them, Gunner Johnson, and locked him in the hotel. He lost three dead in the hotel fight and the rest of the gang got away."

"Which means you must have Gunner still in jail, right, Sheriff?"

"Matter of fact, I don't, Andrews. Handshoe didn't take time to turn him over to me. He left him at the hotel, and went after the other five. One of the gang circled around, came back to the hotel, and broke Gunner out. They rode hell-for-leather back to the main fight up river."

"So the whole Willy Boy Gang got away free and unscathed?" Andrews asked.

"Appears as how. One of Handshoe's men slipped away. Another got paid off and left. He claims they shot one of the outlaws, but he isn't sure which one, or how bad. From what I could tell, they lured Handshoe and his six men into an ambush out there and there was no way to get out."

"Damn! So I head west and keep on their trail."

Sheriff Groller looked up, curious. "You

from that Texas town where they jail broke?"

"Yes."

"Least wise you didn't get killed."

"Willy Boy thought he killed me. You ever been shot in the head, Sheriff Groller?" Seth took off his hat and showed the sheriff his head bandage.

"Hell, Andrews, you're lucky to be alive. Why don't you settle down somewhere and take up farming. Hunting that bunch could cut your life span down some."

"I'm aware of that, Sheriff. Because of me, the Willy Boy Gang has killed almost 30 good men. I don't want to think all of those fine men died in vain. I've got to bring that gang back — riding their horses, or tied over them."

Deputy Sheriff Seth Andrews put on his hat and walked out of the office. He rode west along the river, looking for the site of the ambush. With any luck there could be some blood still on the ground, and if he was lucky, some hoof prints moving west and north in the soft soil along the river.

He had to do some real tracking now to follow up on the outlaws.

CHAPTER
THREE

Friday afternoon at 2:55 P.M. the Willy Boy Gang members began to filter into the only bank in Rock Springs. They wore their cowboy traveling clothes and kerchiefs.

Willy Boy was the last one in the door. It was a minute before three. The owner-manager of the bank, Charles Kaufman, stood near the door looking at his watch. He sighed, pulled down the blind on the glass panel in the door, and closed the twist lock securing the door.

Just then, Willy Boy pushed him against the wall, his six-gun in the man's chest.

"Don't say a word. Close your eyes," Willy Boy hissed. "Now, do it!" Willy Boy shouted.

There were three customers in the bank, two women and a man. Willy Boy spun the president around to face the wall and tied his hands behind him with a piece of rawhide thong. He whipped a neckerchief from his pocket and tied it around Kaufman's eyes as a blindfold. That done, he pushed the president down to the floor, out of sight of the front window, and tied his feet with another piece of rawhide thong.

The gang pulled up their own neckerchiefs to cover their faces when Willy Boy shouted. The Professor vaulted the low partition into the back part of the bank and leveled his six-gun at the bookkeeper. Quickly he blindfolded him, gagged him, and pushed him to the floor.

Johnny Joe had been next in line at the teller's window. At Willy Boy's command, he lifted his neckerchief mask in place, his revolver covering the teller. The Professor ran over. He blindfolded the teller, gagged him, and tied him hand and foot.

He returned to the bookkeeper and tied him.

Eagle and Gunner were dealing with the three customers.

"Face down on the floor!" Eagle barked at them through his mask. The women's eyes widened. Then they lay down on the floor. The man hesitated until Gunner grabbed him by the shoulders and squashed him to the floor. The three were quickly gagged, blindfolded, and tied hand and foot.

The Professor had cleaned out the teller's cage but had not found a lot of cash there. He could find no secret cash drawer below the partition.

He went into the vault. It had no alarms he could detect. Soon the whole gang was emptying out drawers of gold coins, putting stacks of greenbacks into the white cloth sacks the Professor had supplied.

"That it?" Willy Boy asked.

The Professor rattled drawers, looked into compartments, and then kicked a box on the floor. He grinned. It had been ready to send on the railroad express car, he guessed. It held another half-dozen bundles of $20 bills and two heavy sacks of gold coin. They distributed it among themselves. Then they checked the people they had tied up. One man had worked his gag loose.

Eagle tied it tightly in place again. The six of them went to the back door, they pulled down their neckerchief masks, and patted them in place. Willy Boy checked each one as they waited at the back door. They left one at a time, at 30-second intervals, turning and waving at the door as they went outside. Their acting had no audience, but they couldn't know that. They walked back to the hotel using three different routes and met in Willy Boy's room, everyone grinning.

"It was too easy," Eagle said. "Where's the fun?"

"The fun is in spending the money, crazy Indian," Willy Boy teased.

They put the money all in one big canvas sack saved from the last robbery. They wandered down to the street, then split up, each enjoying a beer in a different saloon and waiting for the discovery of the bank heist.

It was almost an hour before the teller freed himself of his bindings in the bank and raced into the street.

"The bank's been robbed!" he screamed. He ran down the boardwalk and barged into the sheriff's office.

Men and women came out of stores and saloons, fancy women from their cribs, or stared out windows.

The Sheriff went sprinting down to the bank and rushed in the front door with the teller. The crowd increased; men ran up to the bank and banged on the door. People began to yell they wanted their money from the bank.

It was ten minutes before Charles Kaufman, the bank president, came out.

"We want our money!" someone shouted.

"Was you really robbed? How much did they get?"

"You said our money was safe."

The banker lifted his hands.

"Your money is safe. I guaranteed it, didn't I? I just don't have any right now. Bear with me for a day or two. I'm sending a man to Laramie on the four-thirty train to cash in some stocks I own, and I'm sure I'll have enough to cover everyone's deposit. Worst thing you can do right now is make a run on the bank.

"Bear with us for two or three days and we'll all be back to normal. Of course, my private accounts in banks in Laramie and Chicago will be drastically reduced. But your money is safe!"

People were somewhat satisfied. The banker went back into the bank. A few kept yelling that they needed money now, but others grinned, saying they were damn glad they had kept their cash money in the mattress.

Johnny Joe laughed and shook his head, then walked into the nearest gambling hall. He stared at the cashier as he handed him a 20 dollar bill. "You have enough cash to cover all the chips you've sold this afternoon?" he asked.

"Yeah, I do now," the cashier said and

grinned. "Just joking, friend. Got plenty to cover the chips. We don't use the bank. Got our own safe."

Johnny Joe nodded, went to a table, and sat in on a quarter-limit poker game. Willy Boy had warned them not to make a big splash by spending money or gambling for high stakes.

He played poker for two hours, won almost $20, and cashed in. On the street he saw the Sheriff's posse gathered. He watched the ten men sitting nervously on their horses. Some had pistols, some rifles. He even saw one man carrying a breech-loader.

The Sheriff talked to them in a loud voice.

"Men, we have two hours til dark. Let's use it. The varmints that robbed the bank was either three or seven — the witnesses can't be sure. They were blindfolded. We think they headed south, but we're not sure. I got two scouts out now riding a circle around town to pick up their tracks.

"Won't be no problem finding three to seven sets of hoofprints hightailing it out of town. I don't want anybody getting hurt. We find them, we close in slow and careful. Want to take them in their camp if we can.

Any you men in the army, either damn side?"

Four held up their hands.

"Good. You lead the rest of the men. Absolute fire control. Nobody shoots unless I give the word. We want these bastards alive, if we can get them. When I say shoot, you shoot. When I say stop, you damn well better cease firing."

The sheriff, a short man with a handle-bar moustache glared at the men again. "All right, we're as ready as we'll ever be. Let's ride." He turned his horse and led the posse out to the south.

Willy Boy turned to the cowboy standing beside him.

"They really going to chase the bank robbers?" Willy Boy asked.

"Damn right, sonny. Chase them and bring back all our money. The ranch owner I work for had five thousand dollars in there. Hope to hell it wasn't all of his cash. Wonder if he's gonna pay up first of the month as usual?"

The Professor had walked down the street until he stood directly across from the bank. He lit up a cigar and leaned against the hardware store, a pair of spectacles perched on his nose.

Two men came out of the store. One

seemed to be the proprietor.

"Hell no," he said. "I didn't see nothing. People go in and out right up to closing time at three o'clock. I don't stand here watching the damn bank all day. I didn't notice nothing unusual. If that old fart Charles Kaufman has lost our money, I'm gonna hang him myself."

"Said he's got some stocks he'll sell in Laramie," the second man said. He looked prosperous in his suit and bowler.

"Figured he had all his money here. Know he bought up about half the town. Course, he'd have to sell some of the buildings to pay off the depositors even then. We'll wait and see. Nobody's gonna make a run on a bank that don't have any cash money at all."

The Professor knocked the ash off his cigar and wandered up the street. He hadn't spent such an enjoyable afternoon since he threw that pip-squeak cheater off the *Mississippi Belle* almost three years ago. Now that had really made a splash, even if they had been tied up in port at the time.

Half a block down the street, the Professor found a chair in front of the saddle shop. He tilted back against the wall and listened to the people of Rock Springs.

A dance-hall girl in a frilly dress walked

by. She held on to a cowboy and was almost crying. Tears had slipped down her face and left tracks.

"Darlin'," she cried, "I had most a hundred dollars in that old bank. I'll never see it again. I know to God I'll never see it. I'm broke and busted again. What am I going to do?"

They stopped a minute and he rubbed one of her breasts. "We'll think of something to do upstairs," said the cowboy, "and a crisp five-dollar bill will help make you feel better again."

"Five? Glory! I ain't never had more than three. Come on before you change your mind." The two almost ran back to the Purple Parrot, a house of pleasure three doors down.

A man in a black suit and a turned-around collar came down the boardwalk slowly, talking with another man in a suit.

"Yes, I know, Brother Barkley. We had all of our church-building-fund in the bank, over six hundred dollars. But we will survive. We'll just work a little harder and start over. Remember, God will provide for his laborers in the fields."

"Amen," the Professor said, watching them walk away. From the other direction a small man came running, trying to dodge a short whip wielded by a large woman. She screamed at him and swung the whip, missing him most of the time, but bringing a wail of pain when it found flesh.

"Idiot! I told you not to put our hard-earned money in that flimsy bank. Never did trust that fancy-talking banker. I'm gonna take every dollar out of your hide, you miserable worm!"

The man did a sudden turn, darting in front of a team of mules. The woman had to wait while the man ran full speed up the alley and out of sight. When the team of mules and freight wagon passed, the woman looked down an empty alley.

"And don't come back!" she bellowed.

By arrangement, the six members of the Willy Boy Gang met that night at two separate tables at the Bakery Cafe. It was the same tent restaurant where Willy Boy had eaten the night before. They paid little attention to each other inside. But in the alley, while waiting for the outhouse, they agreed it was time to move on.

"It's been interesting to see the reaction of a town after a bank robbery," the Professor said. "But I've seen enough."

Willy agreed. They would ride out in the morning after a late breakfast, leaving in pairs.

They finished supper and came on the street just as the Sheriff's posse returned to town. They were dusty and appeared angry.

"Get the bastards?" someone shouted to the Sheriff.

He turned to the caller. "Hell no! Didn't even find any tracks. Could have been on the afternoon train for all I know. Might have ridden out one at a time. Might even be on the street right now, listening to me and laughing. Christ, being sheriff didn't used to be this damn hard. We'll take another look in the morning."

Ten minutes later, the gang assembled in Willy Boy's room. They closed the blinds, locked the door, and stuffed a chair under the handle. Then the Professor counted the take from the bank job.

He stacked the currency by denomination, counted it, and made an entry on a small pad of paper. The coins were in tens on the dresser. At last he totaled up all the figures on the pad.

He looked up. "Six thousand, two hundred and twenty four dollars. Twice what I thought we might get. They had no business keeping that much cash in a town this size."

"The box on the floor," Willy Boy said.

"Looks like they were getting ready to send that cash out on the train."

"We'll take it for them," Eagle said. They all laughed.

Willy Boy rubbed his jaw. "We'll each take a thousand and keep the two hundred and twenty four in the company fund. Any objections?"

The Professor divided the money, giving each man gold coins and paper money. Juan asked for four $100 bills.

"I'll send them to my people in Mexico," he said. "The large bills get through the mail without notice by the banditos who handle the mail. No, instead I will send it to my uncle on the American side of the border. He will take it to my Juanita."

"Food supplies?" Willy Boy asked.

Juan looked up. "We need some. How far to the next town?"

"We'll follow the tracks for about 40 miles or so, then turn northwest to Kemmerer about another 40 miles. So we want food for two days. Juan, you can pick it up in the morning." He handed the Mexican a $20 bill from the company money. "This is where our company money goes."

They all laughed.

Willy watched them. "Remember,

tonight nobody spends a lot of money or gambles wild. Nothing to attract attention. In Kemmerer we can blow it out. The local sheriff isn't convinced the bank robbers left town. He might be smarter than he looks, and we don't want any problems with the local law."

That night, Juan wrote a letter to his Juanita. Gunner stayed in his room. Johnny Joe hit a new poker game. He put $50 on the table and won two hundred more.

In another saloon, the Professor got into a philosophical discussion about the origins of man with one of the fancy ladies. She swore up and down that the world was created in seven days, some four thousand years ago. The Professor laughed and asked her about human bones found in ancient tombs. She scoffed and asked him if he'd seen those bones.

The Professor admitted that he hadn't. He asked her, in turn, if she had ever seen God. They continued the discussion upstairs in her crib and later back to the table. At one o'clock they both gave up, each thinking the other had lost the argument.

Willy Boy drank a beer at a saloon he hadn't been to before, down at the far end of town. He played a game of solitaire and won. The youngest whore in the place came over and bet him two dollars he couldn't win again.

"Sorry, but I don't bet with ladies," Willy Boy said.

She grinned. "My name is Susie and I'm no lady, so you can bet with me."

Willy Boy looked at her. He knew she was a fancy woman, but she didn't seem much older than he was.

"How old are you?" he asked.

"Eighteen."

"Bullshit. Maybe you're sixteen. How long you been. . . ."

"A whore? Oh, little over a year. I'm not complaining. It's no fun starving and being cold. I've been both and I don't like either." She grinned and dimples hit both cheeks. She had soft blonde hair, cut short and curled, and pouting, little-girl lips that the other whores had painted to look larger. Her deep-blue eyes caught his fancy.

"Is it a bet or not?" Susie asked.

Willy Boy watched her a minute. She wasn't teasing him. Business was slow that night because of the bank robbery. He liked her. He shrugged. "I'm down to four-dollars. It's a two-dollar bet."

They shook hands. He glanced up at her

touch and she smiled, a warm, friendly smile. That was her job, Willy Boy knew.

He put a two-dollar gold piece on the table. She reached down the front of her dress and took two folded dollar bills.

"Still warm," he said, touching the bills.

She laughed softly. "Play, cowboy."

He dealt out the game of seven-card solitaire and went through the deck one time. He had only four cards up on two aces when he pushed the cards together.

"I lose," he said. "The two dollars is yours."

"Thanks," she said. No hard-luck story, just one human being talking to another. She glanced at him. "You want to come upstairs with me?"

"Hell yes! But is two dollars enough?"

"Yes. I started at a single. But now I'm more grown up. Come on, the rooms are bigger than lots I've seen and there's a lock on the door."

He hesitated. She smiled. "You've done this before?"

"Yeah, sure. Not a lot, but some."

"You on a ranch around here?"

"Yeah, way out, don't get into town often."

"How old are you?" she asked.

"Seventeen. Be eighteen in two months."

"Then this is a happy birthday present . . . for only two dollars. I charge some of them five."

"I can pay five."

She shook her head. "Five dollars is a week's pay. I won't take that much. Come on, I want to talk. Do you want to talk?"

"Sure, I'm a good talker."

He was sure somebody would yell at them, make fun of him. He had his hand near his six-gun as he walked with her down the saloon. They went through a door at the side of the big room, down a hall and then up steep steps to the second floor. The third door was open, and she went in and waited for him.

The room was about six by eight, with a bed, a small dresser and a picture beside a calendar on the wall.

"We each have our own room," Susie said. "Nobody else uses them. I like it that way." She began undressing slowly and he watched her, fascinated.

"Tell me about yourself. Where is your family? Why are you way out here in Wyoming?"

He began talking and it seemed he couldn't stop. He told her about his mother dying and his father getting shot and how he had to run for his life.

"So I'm hunting the bounty hunter who killed my pa," he said. She began undressing him and he hardly noticed. He went on talking, telling her he had been robbed in Kansas City and sent to jail, and how he got out and rode away. He didn't say anything about shooting anyone.

They came together softly, gently, and he was amazed how tender and concerned she was. Afterwards, they talked some more.

She was from San Francisco. Her mother got drunk one night and lost her downtown. She was ten years old then. She had wandered around for two days before a kind lady took her in. The woman tried to find her mother, but the flat where they had lived was empty, and no one knew where her mother had gone.

Susan stayed almost four years with the woman. Then one day she had an argument with her and ran away. A man found her. He told her he would take care of her, and help her earn lots of money.

"So I become a whore at 13. He charged 20 dollars for me because I was so young, and lots of men liked me that young." She sighed. "I don't know why I'm telling you all of this, it's no worry of yours. Everyone has troubles of their own."

"Is your real name Susan?"

"Yes."

"I like that. Susan, are you saving money to go back to San Francisco, or somewhere else?"

"Yes, I have $20 already."

"Good. I hope you get what you want."

He took a $20 bill from his pocket and put it in her hand. "Now you have $40 for train fare." He bent down and gently kissed her cheek, then slipped out of the room and down the stairs. A small tear rolled down Susan's cheek.

CHAPTER

FOUR

Willy Boy and Juan bought trail food the next morning at the big framed tent that served as the general store. They bought enough food for two men on a six-day ride, and the clerk didn't raise an eyebrow. When it was packed away in the canvas tote bag, Juan paid with a $20 bill. The clerk looked at it hard before accepting it.

"Still rather have gold," he said. He gave back change in paper. "Give paper, you get paper," the clerk said. Juan nodded and they carried the food sack out to the horses.

As Willy and Juan rode slowly down Main street to the west, they met the Sheriff's posse forming up in front of the jail. They paused to listen to the sheriff.

"Men, we've still got no leads, but we're moving out to take another look. I still figure on south, but I sent telegrams both ways along the tracks alerting the sheriffs there to be on the lookout for three to seven men riding together. If we find a bunch of cowboys coming to town, we'll sort that out quick.

"Keep your eyes open. We're going east this morning to check the trails and the ranches. Everybody got weapons?"

A moment later the Sheriff gave a call and the ten-man posse rode out heading east.

"So that's how it's done," Juan said. "I've never seen a posse head out of town before." He laughed. "Especially one hunting for me."

They rode slowly along the street, picking up the pace a little past the last house. They met the other four men five miles outside of town, to the west along the Bitter River. None of them encountered any trouble leaving town.

"Posse went to the east, so looks like we won't have any palaver with them," Juan said.

"Damn," the Professor brayed. "I wanted to have a discussion with the Sheriff on the benefits of bank robbery over the less remunerative aspects of stage coach banditry."

They all laughed.

"What in hell did he say?" Johnny Joe asked, and they all laughed again.

They set out to ride 40 miles a day. The route led downstream along the Bitter River to the west, generally in line with the Union Pacific tracks. There had been a wagon road there long before the railroad surveyors picked the route as the best right-of-way.

It was slightly after midday when they came to the Green River, where the Bitter dumped into it and flowed south. They rode upstream a half mile along the Green. They found a place to ford the river; the water was down low since it was now August.

Just at sundown they came to a spot along the tracks where the steel rails angled away to the southwest. They had heard only one train on the tracks, and when it came heading west they had dropped into a low place on the trail to be out of sight while it passed.

"This is as far as we go due west," Willy Boy said. "Feller back at the freight office said there's an old wagon road that angles northwest here up toward Kemmerer. Not a big place, but right near the border of Idaho Territory."

They made camp on a small stream heading for the Little Muddy River, and well away from the tracks.

They had chewed jerky and drunk water for their noontime meal and now looked forward to a real feast. Juan made a campfire, boiled a big pot of potatoes with skins, and opened three cans of green beans purchased at the store. He fried up big steaks sliced from a cured ham. That, with slabs of fresh bread from the bakery and coffee, filled up the hungry travelers.

After the meal, just as it started to get dark, Eagle took a small ride.

"Making a little scouting trip," he said. "Don't like the idea of this wide-open country without some kind of watch being set, or at least patrolled." As darkness fell he took his horse and left.

Willy Boy shrugged. "Take a ride if you want. I've had enough of forking that nag of mine for today."

Eagle rode along their back trail, and about half a mile away he gained a small rise. He could see the railroad tracks and the steaming, smoking eastbound train as it clattered and roared through the night, about a half mile south of him.

When the train passed, he sat on his horse listening to the night. There were animals and birds here he had never heard. Cousins of those he knew, perhaps. He heard what he was sure was a pair of eagles screaming at each other in a tall cotton-wood tree near the big river.

Eagle sniffed the air. The gentle wind blowing to the east brought the pungent smell of smoke from their cooking fire. He looked in that direction but couldn't see it. Most of his attention went back along their trail.

There was no sign of a winking fire. He couldn't smell any smoke downwind of them. He heard no human voices, no thud of horses' feet on the high plateau sloping upward on two sides into the mountains.

Eagle got off his mount and lay on the ground. He closed his eyes and let his mind dart back to those wonderful days as a child nurtured in the Comanche way of life on the Texas plains. They had been fine years, wonderful years. He had learned everything he could want from his parents and the older men in the band.

A night bird shrilled, calling its mate. Eagle sat up and saw its fleeting dark shadow cross the full moon. He knew there were Indians in this area. They might be Shoshoni, or maybe some wandering Cheyenne. If they met any, he could talk with them in sign language, if nothing else. His Comanche language was much the same as some of the Plains tribes, he wasn't sure which ones.

Eagle continued to watch and listen for an hour, but heard nothing out of the normal. He rode back to the camp, picketed his mount, and slipped off the saddle. Then he lay down in his blankets. All of the men were sleeping. Only the Professor roused, his six-gun up quickly.

"Easy," Eagle said softly. The Professor recognized his voice.

"Anything doing out there?"

"Nothing but natural creatures of the Great Spirit."

"Good," the Professor said, and went back to sleep.

The next morning, they had bacon sandwiches with three fried eggs each; Juan used up the whole supply of eggs that he had been protecting all the first day. Coffee topped the meal and they rode just after sunup.

They had been moving along the stage road when they saw a dust trail far ahead. It seemed to be coming directly towards them. They went off the wagon road into a stand of brush and aspen, with a single cottonwood skying above them.

They waited for the dust to turn into something. A half hour later a stage coach pulled by four horses appeared. It was a full coach, with two passengers on top hanging on with all of their strength.

As it passed, Johnny Joe spoke up. "I didn't know there was a stage up this way. We could have ridden the damn stage."

"Sure, and had three sheriffs and six deputies waiting for us at Pocatello. Not a chance we get on a stage coach anywhere around the county where we busted that bank open."

"You ever robbed a stage, Willy Boy?" the Professor asked as he pushed his hat back on his forehead.

"No. Not enough cash involved for the risk. Besides, you can't tell who might be hiding inside that coach."

"Could be something valuable in the strong box, though," the Professor went on. "I hear the banks get their money on the stage coach in these out-of-the-way spots."

"Maybe, maybe not," Johnny Joe said. "How far we got to go today?"

Willy Boy said about 40 miles and they headed out. It was just after a quick stop for bread, jam, and coffee for midday repast when Eagle stood up suddenly.

"Nobody make a move," he said sternly. "No gunplay, or we're all dead. You men

54

hear me? Let me take care of this. I should be able to talk to him."

A lone Indian sat on a horse 20 yards away, where a slight bank rose next to the creek. He simply sat there watching them.

Eagle slowly shucked off his blue shirt, pulled a headband from his pants, and put it around his black hair. He walked casually forward toward the Indian. He had not removed his gunbelt and still carried the six-gun.

He held his right hand in the air, his smaller two fingers bent over and held with his thumb. It was the universal sign for 'friend' in the tribes, and Eagle was sure the man would recognize it.

The Indian on the horse returned the sign, dropped off his war pony, and walked to meet Eagle. The two signed, and spoke a few words that each knew. As they talked 25 Indians silently rode up on their horses and came into sight, completely surrounding the five men near the small fire. None of the men drank any of the coffee. No one wanted another chew of his bread and jam.

The two Indians talked and signed for five minutes. Then they dropped to the ground, sat cross legged, and continued their meeting. After another five minutes they rose and made more signs. The warrior leaped on his pony's back, gave a yell, and rode down and out of sight.

The other Indians followed him out of view, into the brush in back of the small rises in the ground.

Eagle watched them go. He walked back to the camp fire, sat down, and stared at it for a moment.

"They are Cheyenne, a long way from home. The buffalo hunting has been bad this year. The warrior was Deer Killer. He asked if we had seen any buffalo.

"I told him there had not been a single giant beast. I suggested he go northeast, toward the great mountains. The buffalo would be feeding closer to the mountains, before they find a wooded place to winter where the snow would not be so deep."

Willy Boy wiped a line of sweat off his forehead. Half a dozen times while the Cheyenne warriors surrounded them, he had wanted to draw his six-gun and start firing. Now he looked at Eagle with more respect. "How'en hell you learn to speak the Cheyenne lingo?"

"Some of the Cheyenne words are the same as Comanche. The rest we did with sign language. I used to know many more words in signing."

"Christ, I figured we were all pincushions," the Professor said. "Those savages had three arrows in their right hand, and those short, deadly little bows in their left. We might have got off one shot each before we would have been stuck like hogs in a killing chute."

"Amen to that," Juan said. "You were very *simpatico* with the Cheyenne warrior."

"He was the point man, the bait for us. If we had killed him, they would have wiped us out and taken our horses and guns. Just because they're on an early fall buffalo hunt, is no reason they wouldn't pick up a few spare horses and guns. I talked Deer Killer out of it. I said they would lose six or seven warriors, and gain only six horses. It was not a good trade. The second man in the band agreed.

"Deer Killer said there was a white-eye ranch ahead about half a day's ride. It is very strong, 30 men there with rifles."

"Will the Cheyenne bother us again?" Johnny Joe asked.

"No, not if we are only passing through. They don't like to see the white-eyes come in and settle on their hunting grounds. Then they get angry and declare war on all white-eyes. Right now they are too concerned with finding the herds of buffalo.

They are a big band with 30 warriors, 120 to 135 people. They will need two buffalo for each family to last them through the winter."

"This close to the railroad they won't find a lot of buffalo," Willy Boy said. "The engines scare them, and the ones that hang around get wiped out by the damn buffalo hunters and their Big Fifty cannons."

They had finished their interrupted meal. Gunner was on his horse first. "Let's ride," he said. "I want to sleep in a real bed tonight in that little town."

They soon picked up the small river that flowed to the northwest. According to Willy Boy, this river should lead them directly to Kemmerer.

"Still want to knock over a stage coach," the Professor said. "Hell, just to say we've done one. So we don't get rich, so what? We'll pick one heading the opposite way we're going, so it'll be a long time before the hold up is reported. By that time we'll be in the next county, or the next territory. No problem that way."

"I'll think on it some," Willy Boy said, and picked up the pace moving down the now clearly defined stage road. It was easy riding and they made good time.

Eagle soon noticed that there were no

ten-mile swing stations along here for the stage. He told Willy Boy.

"The horses must have to last for 20 miles, which is why they were moving slower than most," he said. "I figure there'll be a swing station or maybe a stage station stop up here another six or eight miles."

There was. They made a mile wide swing around it to make it harder for any sheriff following them and then regained the roadway.

Ten miles farther northwest they saw a cloud of dust in the east. As they watched it, the milling mass of dark brown rolled closer to them.

"Buffalo," Eagle said. "My god, look at them, there must be five thousand in that herd."

The animals were moving at a steady pace away from them, heading northeast toward the mountains, in the same direction Eagle had told the Cheyenne to ride.

"Your Cheyenne buddies are going to eat well tonight," Juan said.

Eagle grinned. "Yeah, yeah. And I made a friend for life if we ever run into that band of Cheyenne again. Knowing where the buffalo herd is, can turn a lowly warrior into leader of the band. Chief, you white-eyes would call him."

"You're a chief with me, Chief Eagle," the Professor said. They all laughed and Eagle grinned. They settled down, riding away from the buffalo and northeast toward Kemmerer, Wyoming.

CHAPTER

FIVE

The Willy Boy Gang rode singly into Kemmerer over a three-hour period. They registered at the only hotel in town. For anyone watching the village closely, the six men had no connection except they had arrived the same afternoon.

Two came in from the western side to confuse anyone on the alert for a group of men.

They had decided to put their horses in a livery and spend a day or two or three in this small town, before moving on toward Poctatello and then Boise. There was no great hurry.

Eagle said his people had been dead for six years. Another week or two wouldn't make much difference.

The Professor checked through the wanted posters in the Sheriff's office. It was located on the ground level at the Lincoln County Courthouse. The man in charge was a willow switch of a kid, no more than 23, who claimed to be the elected sheriff.

"Wanteds? Yes, Sir. I try to keep up on them. We don't get all of them out here, they do back in Cheyenne. This is a little out of the way for the big time outlaws." He had an open, pleasant face with soft blue eyes and a long nose. His smile more than offset the long proboscis.

He pulled open a drawer and lifted out a stack of wanted posters.

"I try to keep them in order of when they come in," the Sheriff said. "Latest one's on the top. You looking for some particular outlaw?"

"Yep, Curley Matlock. Usually the sheriff in my home state sends wanteds out to places where Curley goes. If you got a wanted, means I got to look a lot harder around here."

The Professor thumbed through the stack twice, but didn't find the poster for the Willy Boy Gang. He nodded.

"Don't guess it's here. Thanks a lot, Sheriff. What's the best eating spot in town?"

"No question. Molly Marshall's Kitchen, half a block down on Main. Beats the other places all hollow."

The Professor thanked him and ambled

out of the office. The air was a little cooler here, for August. He wondered what the elevation was here? Rock Springs had been a little over 6,200 feet. This should be uphill a little toward the Rocky Mountains.

That's where he wanted to be, in the middle of the Rockies, in Denver. He'd give five years of his life to hit that damned Colorado Mountain Bank again. This time with the gang. This time knowing exactly what was inside, where the guards were, and who had the guns behind the counter. He'd blow half of them away with a shotgun and take the place apart.

The Professor leaned against a frame building and thought about it. He'd nearly been killed there two years ago when he and another guy tried to take down the bank. He'd been young and stupid, thinking a fast pistol could do anything. It can't. Not when it's up against a double-barreled shotgun.

Yes, he'd have that bank, but it would be a while before the gang got to it. He could wait. In the meantime he had a good crew. They'd take a bank whenever they wanted to, or needed to.

He still thought about the stagecoach. He wanted that kind of a notch in his rifle stock, just to say he'd done it.

The Professor grinned. Damn, but he was having himself one hell of a good time. A lot more fun than teaching in some one-room schoolhouse somewhere.

He thought of his gang. A strange mixture of men, but it worked. They had been thrown together by chance, and were now bound together by life and death decisions. He knew more about the rest of the men than they knew about him.

He didn't tell them he was wanted in Illinois on a charge brought by a beautiful, pregnant girl. Her father had demanded marriage or $5,000 in damages. The Professor had done at least a $100 in damage to her father's face and teeth before he could no longer stand up. The Professor left that same day for St. Louis, and points farther west.

Yes, a few women, some good sipping whiskey, and a bank to rob, now and again. What more could a man ask for?

Up the street half a block, Juan Romero came out of the general store. He had bought a new quarter-inch rope. He would fashion it into a lasso, and coil it on his saddle to look more like a cowboy. He liked to rope and was quite good at it.

Juan longed for the quiet, peaceful village in Mexico where he was born and grew up, before he crossed the border with his parents into the new Republic of Texas. When Texas became part of the United States things changed.

He had stayed on the land, married a beautiful girl, and had a son Ernesto. Then bad things began to happen and for no good reason he was in jail. He had not wanted to break out with Willy Boy that night. If he had not, Willy Boy would have shot him dead in his cell.

So he had decided to go with Willy Boy, fight off the posse, and bounty hunters, and, as soon as he could, ride back to Mexico to his wife Juanita.

Only now they were getting farther and farther away from Mexico. Would he ever get back to his family? He would send money through his Uncle, who was as honest as a rock. At least his young family would not go without.

He went back in the general store and bought two pair of heavy socks and a spare shirt to roll up in his blankets. An extra shirt would soon come in handy in this high altitude, though it was August.

For one glorious moment he thought of riding away. He had over $2,000 in cash in his money belt, tied securely around his waist under his shirt. It would be enough to live on for five years in Mexico. The wonderful idea gripped him and he hurried out to his horse.

But then he slowed. He was not a *bandito*. He did not want to be a bank robber or a killer. Yet, in his heart, he knew that after riding with Willy Boy, he was both of those things. The night they broke out, he had decided to stay with the gang for a year. That would be support enough. Then, he would ride towards Mexico, no matter where in the United States they might be. He sighed and checked his horse. Then he wandered down the block toward a saloon to get a beer.

Gunner Johnson had registered at the hotel and put his horse in the livery, as instructed. Now he walked down the main street looking for Willy Boy. The town was much smaller than Rock Springs, only two blocks long.

Gunner had seen only two saloons, one hotel, half a dozen stores, and two places to eat. It wasn't much of a town. Gunner towered over the other people on the street. He soon pushed into one of the saloons, ordered a nickel beer at the bar, and looked around.

Willy Boy sat at the first table. Gunner

grinned and headed that way. He knew people called him stupid and slow-witted, but he was as smart as most folks. He just got a little confused and tongue-tied sometimes if nervous or excited. When that happened, he couldn't say exactly what he wanted to say. The words came out wrong. But he was just as smart as anybody else.

He sat down beside Willy Boy and grinned.

"Hi," Gunner said. "Mind if I sit here?"

Willy Boy nodded and they sipped at their beers.

"Enjoy this little town while you can," the short man said softly to Gunner. "In the morning we're going to head out of here, find ourselves a stage coach and see what it's like to take one of them down."

Gunner grinned. "Goddamn!" he said. "Wait'll I tell the Professor."

The next morning they had breakfast and then rode out of town in pairs to the west. Johnny Joe had asked about the stage at the depot. It would be leaving town, heading for Pocatello, about 11 that morning.

Plenty of time. They would find a good spot, well out of town, take down the stage coach, put it out of commission, and then head on up the trail.

About ten miles out of Kemmerer they found a small creek where the stage coach crossed. It was little more than a brushline now, only a trickle of water because of the dry weather in August.

They slowed as they came to it, and they all nodded.

"This is the spot," Eagle shouted.

"Yes, here, they'll have to slow down to get across the creek," the Professor said.

"Besides, we can drag some brush or an old log onto the trail, blocking it," Johnny Joe said. "The driver won't see it until he comes around the little turn right there."

They found a fallen tree, still solid. Using two horses and ropes they dragged it in place, blocking the trail. It took them a half hour. Then they cut brush with their heavy knives and piled it behind the log.

Eagle climbed a cottonwood that towered over the other trees and looked back down the trail.

"Nothing coming for at least five miles," he said. He climbed down. Juan started a fire. They ate ham steaks, finishing what had been left over the other day, and some fresh bread, bought at the town's bakery on the way out. They made large ham sandwiches while Juan poured lots of coffee.

Johnny Joe figured the stage would be there about one o'clock. At 12:30, Eagle went up the tree again and came down grinning.

"I see a dust trail about a mile back. Shouldn't take them more than 15 minutes to get here."

Willy Boy positioned the men in the brush and gave them instructions.

"First, we stop the horses. Gunner, you and Juan take out the left front horse. That's the lead animal. Use your rifles and shoot for the horse's head. It goes down, the rig stops in a jumble of tumbled-around passengers, and the driver falls off the rig.

"We don't kill anybody unless they make us. No sense getting some sheriff all riled up because of a little stage robbery.

"We all fire one round from our pistols into the air as soon as the rig stops. We have our masks up, and order everyone out before we show ourselves."

"I see them coming!" Gunner called.

"All right, now remember, nice and easy. No rough stuff unless they start it, and I don't think they will. We talk as little as possible. I'll yell at them to come out. Stand and deliver, I think is the term."

They crouched behind trees and brush,

as far out of sight as possible from the stagecoach driver's view.

As the stage came closer Willy Boy could see one man on the high seat, the driver. No shotgun guard. He wondered how many passengers.

The gang's horses had been hidden 50 yards downstream, where they would be out of sight, and would not take a wild round.

Now Willy Boy could see the expression on the driver's face. He was bored. He slowed the rig as he approached the stream bed. He'd be almost walking the animals by the time he made the little turn. Then he would see the barricade for the first time.

The horses came closer. Willy Boy would give the signal to shoot the lead horse, so no one would fire too early.

The rig came even with him.

"Now!" Willy Boy thundered. At once two rifles spoke. The lead horse stumbled and went down in the traces. Then the driver saw the barricade, but it was too late. He tried to pull the team to a stop, but the right front horse stumbled when one of the dying animal's legs plunged sideways. Both animals went down, and the team behind them jolted into them, as much as the harness would allow.

The stagecoach stopped with a crash, sending the driver off the high seat and sprawling onto the backs of the fallen horses.

A woman screamed from inside the coach.

Willy Boy lifted his six-gun and fired two shots in the air, and the other five men did the same.

"You inside! All of you. Step out and keep your hands in the air. Driver, you too. Drop that iron and reach!"

He waited a minute.

"Driver get out here, or you're a dead man!"

The driver crawled over a horse that was kicking. The teamster was holding his right arm. He struggled to the side of the stage.

"Get them out of there, driver!" Willy called again.

Three women and one man came down the step from the stage. Two were plump women in their forties. The third was younger and more slender. All wore hats which were now askew.

The man was a salesman wearing a brown suit and bowler. He had crushed the top of the bowler.

"Check it out, number one, from that

side," Willy called.

The Professor grinned. He sprinted from the brush on the far side of the coach, and ran up to it. He looked inside, saw no one else.

"Clear inside," the Professor called.

The men pulled up their neckerchief masks as they came out of the woods and the brush.

"Purses, wallets, jewelry," the Professor said, holding out the man's bowler for their contributions. "No hurry ladies, take your time. Just don't miss any diamonds."

Willy Boy stepped to the top of the coach and pulled the cover back from the driver's box. Usually the driver sat on it with a cushion tied on, and often inside the driver's box was a strong box.

Willy Boy lifted the cover of the driver's box, and yelped in glee. He picked up a tough wooden box, two feet long, eight inches thick and a foot wide. He dumped it over the side to the ground, but it didn't break open.

The driver waved a key. "Nothing inside. Don't break it. Made it myself. Nothing in there but some mail."

Willy Boy took the key and opened the box. The driver was right, just some letters, no cash in them. He locked it and returned the key to the driver.

"Busted my arm," the driver said.

Willy Boy shrugged. "Better get a splint on it so it won't hurt so much."

Willy Boy motioned and the rest of the men faded into the trees, one by one, heading for their horses. Willy Boy told the stage coach people to stay where they were for ten minutes. Someone would be watching them with a rifle. Then he walked into the woods.

A mile down the road they stopped to examine the loot.

"Two diamond rings worth maybe $50 all told," the Professor said. "We got $45 in gold and currency, and one gold watch that I'd like to claim."

Willy Boy shrugged. "Fine with me. Now that, men, is why we don't rob stage-coaches. Too dangerous and not enough loot. Let's ride."

Chapter
SIX

Deputy Sheriff Seth Andrews lifted himself out of the chair and steadied himself. He still felt wobbly when he stood up too fast.

"Thanks, Sheriff Groller. I appreciate your help. From the way the bank people were tied up and the timing of the robbery, I'm certain it was the Willy Boy Gang. One of the men, known as the Professor, is an expert at robbing banks. He usually does it this way — never any gunplay. Any idea which way they headed out of Dodge City?"

"Not a one. They could have boarded the train anytime that day, or three or four days later. I didn't know who to look for. We didn't have any good clues at the time. Hell, our bank ain't never been robbed before."

"These are some of the best outlaws around, Sheriff. Just wish I knew where they're headed. Guess I'll send some telegrams along the tracks both ways, see if any more banks have been robbed. Must be a way to track those bastards."

Seth sent telegrams to the sheriffs of the three railroad settlements within 50 miles in each direction along the tracks. He got back quick answers. No sign of the Willy Boy Gang. No train or stagecoach robberies to report within the last two months.

Seth frowned as he sipped at his coffee in the hotel dining room. So what the hell did he do now? Where did he go? He could try the outskirts of town to see if anyone remembered a group of six riders heading out 13 days ago.

He knew the reaction he would get. Anyway, groups of cowboys came and went out of town all the time. He sipped the coffee. Best coffee he'd had in weeks. Then he snorted. If he was part of the gang, he wouldn't advertise by riding in and out of town in a cluster. He'd have them go in and out, one or two at a time. Damn!

A pair of blue-clad soldiers rode into town and reminded Seth of Fort Dodge. It was only a few miles east out of town. Dodge? He thought a minute, then nodded. He had a cousin stationed there, a Lieutenant. He was younger than Seth. Probably should stop by and say howdy, or his mother would raise old billy hell when he got back to Texas.

That afternoon Seth rode out to the fort. He inquired about Lieutenant Berry. The Officer of the Day grinned.

"Yes sir. Lieutenant Berry works with the Adjutant. Could I show you to his office?"

Ten minutes later Seth leaned back in a chair, and worked on a fresh glass of sippin' whiskey that Lieutenant Philip Berry poured.

"Hell, Seth, ain't seen you for two years. You still down there in Oak Park?"

"Just nearly. You ever see a man who's been head-shot?"

Seth showed him his wound and told him about it.

"So I'm on the little bastard's trail. Seen anything of him around here?"

"Don't get into town much, and not much chance he'd come here. Kind of quiet for us right now. The shoot and kill business is kind of slow."

"You seen any civilians around the fort the last month or so? I'm getting desperate, Phil."

"Civilians," Phil Berry paused, sipped at the whiskey, and stared at the open beams of the ceiling. "Two or three weeks ago seems, there was a civilian talking to Lieutenant Parsons. He's the Adjutant here. Should be a captain, then I could get my first lieutenant rank. Now, what was that guy jawing about?"

He sipped the whiskey again. "I was just going through the office and they was talking. The guy was looking for some army outfit, and Parsons said he couldn't tell him that. But they went on talking.

"Yeah, I remember. The kid was looking for the Fourteenth Cavalry Regiment — the outfit I tried to get into when I got out of West Point. So I perked up my ears. The Fourteenth, damn certain. Why don't I go in and ask Lieutenant Parsons about it. He might remember more details."

"Anything, Phil. I'm grabbing at anything here to stay afloat."

Five minutes later, Phil Berry came out of the Adjutant's office with a grin as wide as an axe handle. He took a pull at the sippin' whiskey.

"Might have found you something, Cousin. Parsons remembered the guy. He was small and looked young, maybe 16 or 18, something like that. The kid said he had a brother in the Fourteenth, and had to find him cause their father died or was bad-off sick. Parsons said he wasn't supposed to give out troop assignments, but he did. The Fourteenth is in Boise. That's Idaho Territory."

"Yeah. Now this civilian, how tall was he?" Seth asked.

"Not tall at all. Lieutenant Parsons said he was a runt, only five-four or five-five. Looked like a kid, but he had a big hogleg on his right thigh, tied down low and solid, like he could use it."

"God damn!" Seth said, and stood up. "That's a near-perfect description of Willy Boy, the bastard who shot me and broke out of my jail. Why would he be going to Boise?"

"Why would he want to know about the Fourteenth?" Phil Berry asked. "It put in lots of time down in Texas chasing Comanche. How would that affect this white kid?"

"Comanche?"

"Oh, hell yes. The Fourteenth had a wild record on tracking down Comanche in North and West Texas, for three or four years, back a ways. They cut up many a tribe of those tough Comanche."

Seth began to grin again. "Yeah, I should have figured it before. One of the gang is called Brave Eagle, a full-blood Comanche. He could be looking for the Fourteenth.

You wouldn't have let Brave Eagle on the fort if he tried to come and ask about the Fourteenth, right?"

"Hell no, we wouldn't let him in. Don't want no sneaky Comanche on this fort."

"So Willy Boy himself came to find out." Seth downed the last two swallows of the whiskey and grabbed for his cousin's hand. "Phil, old cousin, looks like you just saved the day. I'll give your mamma a big hug when I get back to Texas."

"Heading back now, Seth?"

"Christ no! I'm taking off for Boise. Figure I'll ride the train far as I can. You got any maps?"

Twenty minutes later, Seth rode back to Dodge City with a grin on his face. By damn! He had them in his sights. For the first time in a week he felt he might really have a chance to catch up with them.

It was a long shot, but it was the only lead he had. They must be heading for Boise and the Fourteenth. The Indian, Brave Eagle, must have a real hatred for that unit to chase it so far. The Cavalry was known for getting rough with Indians — especially the Comanche, who had terrorized Texas for so long.

It just might have been the Fourteenth Cavalry that had hit Brave Eagle's tribe in

Texas. Might be? Hell, it *had to be!* Seth knew it in his bones.

He was going to ride due north to the railroad tracks in Nebraska at North Platte. He'd try to wrangle a pass from the District Manager for an 800-mile ride west to the middle of Nevada. The train trip would save him about three weeks of hard riding. Maybe he could get ahead of the bastards and warn the fort. . . .

He thought it through again. If Willy Boy and his gang were heading for Boise, they had plenty of money to buy train tickets. If not, they would simply rob another bank. They probably would take the train as well. So he might not beat them to Boise. Maybe they wouldn't ride as far as he did.

They would be in no hurry. Maybe he could make up those 13 days he trailed the gang. Seth set his jaw, pulled his brown hat down firmly on his head, and raced back to Dodge City to get supplies for his ride 220 miles due north. There was no stage heading that direction. He would allow himself five days to make the trip. That was 44 miles a day. Hell yes, he could do that!

That afternoon he put together a trail ride supply sack, making it as light as he could. He talked to the livery man an hour about buying a second horse.

"Want what?" the livery man asked. His name was Josh Bridger, and he had to be in his seventies. He'd run liveries in Dodge and in St. Louis since he was a pup of 13, he had so proudly proclaimed to Seth.

"Got a 200-mile ride up to the railroad. Wondering about a spare horse. Like the Indians do. Ride one and trail one, then ride the other one. Gallop, canter, make some time. Average about seven miles an hour."

Josh took off a black stained, once-white hat and scratched his scalp through his almost vanished hair.

"Need two damn good horses for that. You ain't even got one. You push that nag you got too hard and her left front leg's going out on you. Even you keep her as a spare, it could go. Now I got a horse that you could do 60 miles a day on. Only trouble, it'll cost you $150 for him. Big, rugged stallion."

"A gelding?"

"Hell no. Still got both nuts, and he's a handful, strong as a small ox."

Seth sagged. "That's more money than I got for the whole trip. Forget it. Now what's this hogwash about my line-back buckskin?"

After a half hour of arguing, boasting, and lying, the two men grinned. No deal was made, but it had been a fine horse-trading haggle that they had both enjoyed.

Seth rode out at six-thirty the next morning, right after having a huge breakfast of hot cakes, bacon, eggs, steak, and a whole pot of coffee. He stopped for a hard loaf of bread at the bakery, and then rode north. Most of the time there wouldn't be a road and he'd have to watch for gopher holes. But he'd never broken a horse's leg yet on the prairie, he didn't figure to start now.

It took him six days to make North Platte. He spent half a day arguing with the district manager at the Union Pacific office. He kept yelling that he was a lawman chasing a band of train robbers and it was to the railroad's benefit to get them caught. At last, he wrangled a half-price pass for a two-way trip to Elko, Nevada. He'd never heard of the place. But even if it took two whole days, he'd save three weeks riding on the back of his horse.

He'd never ridden the train before. The conductor guaranteed an average of 25 miles an hour, day and night, unless there was some trouble, like a washed out track or a stray herd of buffalo on the tracks.

"Stop three times a day for food, but you got to eat fast because we allow only 15 minutes at each stop," the conductor said. "Best way is to buy a sandwich and some fruit that you can take on board the train. I don't wait for nobody. You still munching on a big dinner, you got to wait for the next train. One a day, heading west."

Seth settled into the padded seat next to the window and watched in amazement. Nothing could travel 25 miles in one hour. It was against nature. But as he saw the telegraph poles flashing past, he remembered how long it took him on his horse to ride from one to another.

It set him to thinking. At 25 miles an hour, they would travel 250 miles in ten hours. From noon that day, to noon the next day they would go over 500 miles!

Impossible! He didn't believe it. It was just too much to accept.

Seth turned out to be right. They came to a washed-out section of tracks just before Cheyenne, Wyoming. They had to wait for four hours for a crew to repair the tracks. It was a jolting, screeching ride across the repaired roadway. Once the train passed, the crew would make permanent repairs before the eastbound got there.

He got off twice to eat, but found the crowding and pushing at the small restaurants set up in the stations almost worse than not eating at all. He passed the time smoking his pipe and reading a three-day old *Omaha World* newspaper. He was amazed at what was happening in the world.

More minor delays held them up half a dozen times. Once, just beyond Rock Springs, Wyoming, Indians had attacked the tracks. They had torn up a short section, and burned up the ties. The passengers waited eight hours before repairs could be made, and the eastbound train backed up to a siding so they could pass each other on the single rail line across the prairie.

He got off the train at the tiny railroad town of Elko, Nevada. Seth bought a horse and headed north. He had a 150-mile ride to the Snake River and the main trail to Boise. Then another 50 miles to his destination.

Every step of the long ride, Seth prayed he would get to Boise before Willy Boy and his gang. He wanted to warn the soldiers and the banks in town. But most of all, he wanted to track down the gang and kill them wherever he found them!

CHAPTER
SEVEN

There was a trail between Kemmerer and Pocatello, Idaho Territory, but it was not much traveled. Willy Boy and his gang lost it a few times. From Kemmerer they headed northwest, and within two days hit Bear River. That strange little stream rises in the Wasatch Range of the Rockies in Utah, flows northward in Wyoming, then northwest into Idaho Territory.

After a northward flow of almost a 100 miles, it turns south again and dumps into Bear Lake, a huge affair straddling the Idaho-Utah border.

Another fork of the river comes down from the north. An old-timer in Kemmerer told them to pick up the north fork of the Bear and follow it upstream to Soda Springs, Idaho. From there it was a quick 50 miles northwest to Pocatello.

Easier said than done.

There was little along the way except magnificent forests, tall peaks they skirted by following the river, and the grandeur of the Rocky Mountains.

"Why they make these critters so tall?" Gunner asked one day, as they stared up at the top of Meade Peak which lifted more than ten thousand feet, and had a few traces of snow along the southern slope.

"Why?" the Professor asked. "Hell, that's the way I wanted to do it. After I created the Great Plains, I got tired of flat things. So I humped these mountains up with so many rocks on them and I called them the Rocky Mountains."

Gunner looked at him a minute, his face serious, then a grin broke through. He laughed. "Professor, you're joshing me again. Shouldn't do that all the time."

The Professor kicked his mount up to the front of the line of march, and asked Willy Boy when they were going to stop.

"Why?" Willy Boy asked.

"Damnit, I want to take a bath in the river before the sun goes down and I freeze my gonads off. Should be reason enough."

It was a warm day. They pulled in at a flat spot along the Bear River and picked out a camp in a clump of trees. Some alder and willow, Willy Boy thought, but he wasn't sure.

Gunner looked at the Professor, stripping off his clothes.

"Gunner, you going to have a bath, too?"

"Naw. I already had one. Last month sometime."

"Come December you'll probably need another one, Gunner. It's a tough old life."

The next day they paused in a crossroads village called Montpelier. The Professor said the place would soon die out. "No reason for there to be a town here," he said. "No railroad, no trail that goes anywhere important. No big lumber mill, or farming, or cattle raising. Hell, this place will be history in another ten years."

What upset the Professor the most, Willy Boy said, was that the place didn't have a bank.

They had a good meal in a small café but didn't investigate the hotel. Instead, they pushed on toward Pocatello.

When they hit Pocatello, they moved into town one at a time, and registered at the biggest hotel. An hour later, at one saloon, the Professor sat down beside Willy Boy, who was working on his third cold beer.

"Sure, they have a bank here," he said quietly. "I went in for my usual dollar's worth of nickels. The place looks like an army camp. They got an armed guard on the door, and not just some old codger to open and close the door. He's maybe 25 and husky, with two handguns in fast leather on his hips and a shotgun within arm's reach.

"Behind the counter I saw two double-barreled shotguns in quick-grab spots on the wall. One of the two tellers wore a little handgun in a holster attached to his belt.

"I wouldn't even think about going in that place again. I near felt threatened just being there."

"So have a beer on me. This is Eagle's party. We should make it to Boise soon. It's only about 250 miles more. What would you say to us riding the stage the rest of the way?"

They sold their horses, cheered when Johnny Joe said the Sheriff had no wanted poster on them, and then settled down to riding the stage. It was a new experience for some of them. The Concord was the finest of the road, but that still meant a rough-and-tumble ride on unpadded seats.

Three persons sat on the seat facing forward, three on the far one facing the rear, and the last to board the rig had to sit on the middle seat, with no back rest and knees and feet all over the place.

On this trip there were eight passengers.

The six Willy Boy Gang members, and two women who also got on at Pocatello.

The Concord rolled along at an average of eight miles an hour. They stopped every 12 miles to put on four to six new horses, depending on the grade ahead. Every 45 to 50 miles they stopped at a "home" station, where they could get something to eat and make a quick trip to the outhouse. Often the driver would be changed at the home station.

They were somewhere between Pocatello and Twin Falls when they heard a shot. They all looked out the windows. Two men, with pistols out, came riding up behind them.

"Company!" Willy Boy shouted and the gang drew weapons. He told the women to lay down on the floor.

"Two more up front!" the Professor called. He had his Spencer up and pushed out the window. They had just started up a steep rise so the rig had slowed to a walk.

The Professor snapped off the first shot, then the second, and they heard a scream of pain from outside. Three more of the gang in the coach blasted hot lead at the bandits. Two more attackers came up on the side.

Willy Boy knocked the closest one off his

saddle with a round from his Spencer. Johnny Joe had used his long gun as well but missed his man, hitting the horse instead, which went down like a rock.

The other three men in the coach peppered six-gun lead at the stage robbers. After a tense three or four minutes, the last of the robbers turned and rode away into a patch of heavy trees along the banks of the Snake River. Three of the attackers lay dead along the trail, and another had lost his horse.

"Should do it," Willy Boy said. He leaned out the window, then crawled up, and looked over the top of the rig.

"You get hit, driver?" he shouted.

"Damn no," the driver called back. "You boys did some fancy shooting down there. Much obliged."

"Don't mention it," Willy Boy said. He slipped back through the window and sat down on the middle bench.

The others had helped the women sit up again. Both were dusty and rumpled, but smiling.

"Leastwise we're still alive," one of the women said. She was in her forties, the mother of the younger woman. "Land sakes, don't know what we would have done if you boys weren't along. Never too good with a shootin' iron myself. We thank you kindly."

"No trouble at all," the Professor said. "Glad to do what we could. I just didn't cotton to losing my granddaddy's gold watch to a bunch of sidewinder stagecoach robbers."

The younger woman looked up and nodded, then smiled. None of them had talked much yet. Now the girl smiled at the Professor. She was 17 or 18.

"Sir, are you going far? Mother and I will be getting off at Twin Falls."

"Bound for Boise, Miss," he said. "Want to see the state capitol and all."

They talked politely for the next hour until they pulled in at the swing station, and new horses were hitched on.

Willy Boy got down and told the driver that the women folk wanted to use the outhouse, so there was no rush.

"Rush. I got a schedule to keep," the driver blustered.

Willy pulled his six-gun, spun the cylinder, then eased it back into leather. "Driver, I'd figure as how you might be dead or dying back there along the trail if it weren't for the help you got from the passengers. Now I figure a little courtesy for the ladies would be appreciated.

Don't you think?"

The driver watched Willy Boy for the next 20 seconds and evidently saw a touch of wild anger in his eyes. He bobbed his head.

"Yes sir, I reckon we got plenty of time. I thank you greatly for your marksmanship back there when those sidewinders made a try for us. I lost one coach on this run. If I'd been robbed again, I'd never drive another mile for the company."

"Good, why don't you light up a smoke and have a drink of cold water," Willy Boy said. "The ladies will be back directly."

Eagle had watched Willy Boy. He went up to the short young man.

"Willy Boy, you ever decide to go into a new line of work, I want to hire you to sell my genuine Indian tonic and snake oil. We could make a fortune. I'll make it and you'll sell it."

Willy grinned. "Took a shine to that young one. But she never so much as looked at me at all the way. Sometimes I really hate being so short. You suppose I'll do any more growing?"

"Don't suspect so, Willy Boy. Too much tobacco, whiskey, and coffee done stunted your growth early on."

"Guess so. Besides that, my ma was only

five feet tall, and my pa was about five-five. Guess I'm following true to breeding form." He looked up. "Thought all you injuns was little short varmints."

Eagle took a playful swing at Willy Boy who ducked. "Some tribes are short. We fought one band once that had no warrior over five-four. The women were smaller yet. But Comanche are bigger. We had one man in our band who was almost six-four. We called him Tall Fox. He got . . . he didn't make it through that final slaughter."

"How tall was your father?"

"Seemed taller than the mountains to me back when I was 12. Now, as I compare him to Tall Fox, I'd say he must have been about five-ten. He was a warrior, could ride that war horse of his like no other man in our band. He was going to be the leader when White Buffalo stepped down."

"Then the soldiers came?"

Brave Eagle shook his shoulders as he remembered. "Yes. But I don't want to talk about it. I must hold it inside me, to make my anger hot, to make my rifle shoot straight when I find the men who killed my family."

"How will you know them? They all had on uniforms, right? How can you remember them from so long ago?"

"Five or six of them I will never forget. A Captain Two-Guns who led the slaughter, and a sergeant they called Hill. He had a scar on one cheek where no hair grew. Those two, especially, I remember."

The ladies came back from the convenience and boarded. Willy Boy arranged it so he sat beside the young girl. Before ten minutes had gone by, he began talking to her and she responded.

At first Willy Boy was nearly tongue-tied, but gradually she talked about herself and her family in Twin Falls. Twice her mother looked over and frowned, but the young man had been so gallant saving their lives in the robbery, she relented and let them talk.

"And what work do you do, Mr. Williams?" she asked him. He had told her his name was Williams.

"Mostly a cowboy. Right now I'm looking for work. Not a lot of cattle raised in this country. Heading for Oregon. La Grande. I hear there's a lot of cattle over there."

"I don't know, but I hope it turns out well for you."

Then they could think of nothing more to say.

After two swing stations for new horses, they came to the home station for their midday meal. It was beef stew, mostly vegetables and little meat. But they ate it hungrily and had second cups of coffee.

Outside, as they waited for the new driver to check out the harness and the rig, Gunner looked down at Willy Boy.

"I like this stagecoach riding," Gunner said. "Not near as hard as riding a horse all day."

"Just don't get used to it, Gunner. We earn our keep on the backs of horses, and that's the way it'll be most of the time. We should be in Boise by three o'clock tomorrow afternoon."

"When do we sleep?" Gunner asked.

Willy Boy laughed. "Anytime you want to. We won't be stopping. The stage pounds along all night. That's how we get there so fast."

That afternoon they stopped at Twin Falls and let off the two ladies. It was a food station. Willy Boy helped the ladies with their bags to the boardwalk. He seemed reluctant to leave them. Then, a large barrel-chested man with a gun on his hip met the ladies, and hustled them into a buggy.

Willy Boy shrugged as they left. "Too

fancy and highfalutin for the likes of me," he said. The Professor chuckled.

"My boy, women are the downfall of us all. Why do you suppose I quit teaching school. Some damned woman. Now, are you going to get something to eat or not?"

From there on, it was one long try to sleep on the bouncing, jolting Concord stage.

"If I ever take another stage ride I'll buy two good thick pillows," Willy Boy said. "One to sit on, and one to lean against when I want to sleep."

Once, well after midnight, they stopped to change horses and driver. The men slept on but Gunner had trouble sleeping. He'd never tried to sleep all night sitting up before, and he was too long to stretch out in the confinement of the coach. He drifted off toward morning.

About seven A.M. they stopped for breakfast. The six men, now the only passengers, stumbled out to the crude log cabin, ate hotcakes and bacon, and gulped gallons of coffee. Then they were back on board the swaying, bouncing coach.

"I'll never ride in a stagecoach again!" Eagle mumbled as he stared out the window. The side curtain had been rolled up and tied at the top. Now the morning breeze and dust could blow in.

"Somebody shoot me if I ever suggest that we take another stage," Eagle said. Johnny Joe growled at him. Gunner had dropped off to sleep again. Juan Romero laughed at him and stared out the other window. The land was so green. Everywhere green trees, green grass, rivers, and water. Juan had seen two waterfalls already this morning. The country was one large garden plot, well-tended but so over watered it spilled into rivers and streams.

Eagle pounded his fist into his palm. "Why can't we go faster? I want to be in Boise right now. I can almost feel their throats in my hands!"

The Professor watched the Comanche. "Easy now, Chief Eagle. We aren't there yet. Just go slow and be sure of your man. Nothing upsets real hatred as much as killing the wrong man."

Eagle looked up, a flare of anger in his face. Then he took a long, deep breath and let it out slowly. The anger faded.

"Yes, Professor. I know you're right. I've been waiting for this day a long time. I have been robbed of my family, and somebody is going to pay, and pay dearly.

"I'm not sure how many of them will be left. But before I'm done with them, they will wish they had never joined the army. At least, they will wish they had never been on that raid in western Texas."

He looked at the Professor, then back out the window. It was all he could do to keep from sobbing as he thought about that terrible day six years ago, along the Sulphur Springs River at Stony Mountain. He would never forget a single, gruesome, terrifying detail of that morning in June.

CHAPTER

EIGHT

Brave Eagle woke up and looked around the small clearing. They had made a camp a hundred yards from his father's tipi, so they could just see it through the brush and trees along the Sulphur River in northern Texas.

He and his best friend, Long Walk, had pretended they were warriors on a raid against the hated Kiowa. They had struck many coups and returned toward camp with 20 horses! There would be a celebration upon their return.

They had made the little camp just before darkness and had slept there like real warriors, with only one buffalo robe to keep warm with. Now it was morning and the game was over.

He poked Long Walk to awaken him. Both of them had just turned 12 and were hard at work learning to become Comanche warriors. They laughed and yelled at each other now and then, wrestling in the soft grass along the stream.

"Are you hungry?" Brave Eagle asked his friend.

"I'm always hungry," the tall skinny boy said. They stopped wrestling and ran for their tipis. The thrill of the pretend warrior raid was forgotten.

That afternoon Brave Eagle would work with his war pony. So far he had taught the animal to stop on command, using a gentle nudge with both knees.

A warrior had to have both hands free to fight. He couldn't use a hackamore or leather reins to control his pony. Next he would teach the bright little horse to turn, to speed up, to slow down, to do everything a real war pony needed to do. And every command would come from his legs, knees, or feet.

Brave Eagle's father said his young pony was developing nicely. By the time he was fully grown he would be a fine war pony.

There had been a buffalo kill the day before. Twelve buffalo from a scattered herd had blundered close to their camp. The warriors turned hunter and killed six of the beasts before they could run away.

There were only six tipis in their small band of 25 Comanches. Each tipi was awarded one buffalo no matter who had killed it. There would be extra summer meat for all, and what couldn't be eaten today fresh had been cut into thin strips to dry on racks in the sun.

The drying racks were simply a framework of poles with sharpened pegs driven into softer cross rails. The strips of raw meat were hung on the pegs to cure in the sun. All the remaining buffalo meat, not eaten the day of the kill, had to be put on the drying rack. The sun would cure it to prevent spoilage.

Brave Eagle grabbed a piece of roast buffalo from a stick over the cooking fire in his parent's tipi, and ran outside with it. He used his hunting knife from his surcingle to scrape off the burned outside of the meat.

Then he chewed the sweet, well-cooked red meat as he sat on the ground, throwing rocks in the stream.

It was a perfect day. He hoped it would never end. There was plenty of food; he was going to go ride his pony soon; and the sun was warm without being too hot. He would ride his war pony he had named Flying Cloud. When he was tired, he would come back and fall into the river. He would splash the girls and send them away screaming in fright. It was what a young warrior always did.

He still had much to learn before he was admitted to the warrior society. But he was learning. Already he had a strong bow and eight arrows he had made himself. He went on the hunting expeditions with the other hunters.

Last week he had killed a rabbit with one arrow. He had lost another arrow, but he would make a new one to replace it. The band's one arrow maker couldn't be bothered making arrows for the young boys. He had to form, straighten, and put feathers and points on the arrows for the six warriors.

Long Walk ran up to Brave Eagle and pretended to stab him with an imaginary knife. The two boys sprawled in the grass. Then they chased each other down past the tipis, tipping over one small drying rack filled with buffalo strips.

The woman from the tipi had been sitting nearby scraping the hide of a buffalo. She set her mouth, looking at the two boys, as she got up to reset the rack, brush off the strips of meat, and put them back to dry in the warm sun.

Indian children were almost never scolded or punished. They went their own way, did mostly what they wanted to. Gradually they learned that there were certain jobs and duties they must perform to be considered a member of the band.

For the boys, they must learn to be warriors. That was their only job, and it began when they were three years old. As teenagers, they were given the responsibility of watching the herds of ponies the warriors owned. Sometimes they would serve as lookouts if an attack was suspected. But mostly they watched the warriors, learned the skills of riding, shooting their bows, knife fighting, and throwing knives and war axes. Their business was killing; it must be learned before anything else.

Brave Eagle and Long Walk tired of their pretend raid on the village and ran to find their ponies.

Neither of them heard the 50 men in the U.S. Cavalry Able Troop of the Fourteenth Regiment as they rode up. Now they sat in the heavy woods just down from the small camp.

Captain Two Guns Riley stood in his stirrups on his black gelding and watched the small camp.

"Remember men, these are not hostiles. We have been told they will come peacefully into the reservation. There will be no weapons fired." He frowned. "Of course, if one of the hostiles does fire at you, any man is obligated to defend himself, in any way possible."

He moved his 50 men forward on a company front. The men were spaced eight to ten feet apart in a long line, facing the village just across the small stream. There was a meadow on his side. The soldiers were spotted at once by the people in the village.

White Buffalo, the leader of the small band, quickly caught his war pony and rode out to meet the Pony Soldier. They faced one another six feet apart.

"We have come to take you to the reservation," Captain Two-Guns Riley said. His Kiowa scout translated to the Comanche leader.

White Buffalo looked surprised. "When we talked before, you said it would be for two moons, just before the winter snow. We have not yet made the fall hunts for our winter food supply."

Captain Two-Guns Riley shook his head. "No. The agreement was for two weeks, not two moons. There are four weeks in a moon. Set the old boy straight."

The interpreter gave White Buffalo the news. His shoulders slumped. He looked at the 50 Horse Soldiers holding their rifles and carbines, and he nodded.

"We will begin to take down our camp. We will be ready to travel in three hours."

"Make it faster, if you can," the captain said, and went back to talk to his men.

White Buffalo rode to the camp where the other five warriors and their families had gathered. Quickly he told them they must break camp to leave. At once the women began taking down the tipis. It was their work to take down the tipi poles and pack up all of their belongings on travois made from them. They had only three hours to do it.

Two of the warriors told White Buffalo it was not right.

"We have not done our fall hunt. What will we eat this winter?"

"The Great White Father will give us beef and corn to eat," White Buffalo told them.

Short Spear did not like the answer. He sulked, went off into his tipi, and took out all his weapons. He would not trust them to his woman. He had two wives and 20 horses. Now he was being sent to a reservation he could not leave. He threw his spear into a tree and bellowed in rage.

Two of the Horse Soldiers on that end of the line looked at him nervously. They had lifted their carbines from the holding rings on the saddle and watched the Indian.

Around the camp, the women began to take down the tipis — the long poles coming out first. The young girls helped pack things. The teenager boys ran to herd the horses, and help the warriors with their war ponies so they could ride to the new camp.

Most of the children did not know where they were going. They did what they always did when moving. The girls helped the women, who did all the work. The men and boys rode their ponies around the camp, as if protecting it from an enemy attack.

Short Spear went inside his tipi. When he came out he had a rifle. He ran toward the Horse Soldiers, lifted the rifle and fired. His bullet hit a corporal in the shoulder pounding him off his horse.

The man beside the downed cavalryman returned fire, killing Short Spear. The sound of gunfire spread like wildfire as the cavalrymen up and down the line began to shoot. They fired into the tipis, at the warriors who rode their horses, and at the women and children.

The women screamed. One small girl took a bullet in the side of the head showering blood over her mother and brothers, who bellowed in terror and fled for the trees.

"Who started shooting?" Captain Two-Guns bellowed.

"They did, sir!" two or three soldiers yelled back.

"Then don't let them get away. Gun down the bastards!"

The shooting intensified as the army unit with Spencer repeating rifles tore through the camp, firing at everyone who moved.

Brave Eagle and Long Walk were half way to the rope corral, where the horses were kept when not grazing, when they first spotted the cavalrymen near their village. The boys dropped into the brush and grass, playing at being warriors. How better to play-fight against the hated cavalry than when they were actually in sight.

They had slithered through the thick growth to the edge of the stream where they had a better look at the Horse Soldiers.

"So many of them!" Long Walk whispered.

"They're talking with White Buffalo," Brave Eagle said. He was a month older than Long Walk and sometimes talked down to him. "It will be all right. They are talking, not shooting."

"Should we go on and ride our ponies?" Long Walk asked.

"No. We wait here to see what the white-eye soldiers do first," Brave Eagle said.

They waited as the leader of their band returned to the small camp and talked to the warriors. The men seemed unhappy but they went to their tipis. Soon the whole camp was a busy place, as the women began to ready for a march.

"We're leaving this place," Brave Eagle said.

"Why? We only arrived a few days ago."

Brave Eagle shook his head. "Doesn't matter, the tipis are coming down. We should get our ponies and ride protection." But Brave Eagle didn't move. He was watching Short Spear who was stalking up and down outside his tipi. He saw the strong warrior take his spear and throw it hard at the cottonwood tree.

"Short Spear is angry," Brave Eagle said.

They watched him as he went into his tipi which already had lost three of its tall poles. He came out with a rifle and ran toward the soldiers.

Brave Eagle didn't believe what he saw. Short Spear ran toward the line of soldiers, then stopped and fired. There was a pause as the warrior tried to load in another round. Then two shots came from the soldiers. Short Spear staggered backwards and fell into the leaves, blood gushing from a wound in his neck.

There was another pause in the sound of rifles. Then the shooting came again, this time every man down the line began firing into the village.

"No!" Brave Eagle shouted, but his voice was washed away by the roar of the rifles. He saw no warrior return fire. One of his aunts picked up her baby and ran toward the woods. Rifles cracked and the woman spun around, a bullet in her chest. She dropped the baby who tried to crawl.

Three Horse Soldiers charged through the camp. One of the horses, crowded by another, stepped on the small human form. The heavy horseshoe smashed through the baby's head, cutting it in half.

Brave Eagle shouted again, but he already knew that there were few alive in the village.

He saw someone running toward him. A woman with a two year old in her arms, hid behind a tipi for a moment. She looked behind, then sprinted for the woods. A soldier, who had lost his hat, spotted her. He rode toward her with his pistol out. He had bright red hair, and he laughed as he fired, twice missing her.

He was almost on top of her and with his next round he killed the baby in her arms. She stared at the small body with a .45 through his chest, the small lungs struggling to breathe. Then he died.

The woman turned and screamed at the soldier.

"Mother!" Brave Eagle whispered as he saw the woman's face, clearly now. "Mother run!" he screamed. The red-headed trooper heard his cry, then turned and shot his mother in the face. She fell backwards, her hands trying to cover the bloody spot where her right eye had been.

The trooper rode up and shot her again in the heart. He laughed as he reloaded his pistol eying the woods where he had heard the Indian voice.

Tears streamed down Brave Eagle's cheeks. His mother, his brother, both dead! What could he do now? He couldn't fight a whole band of the Horse Soldiers.

Long Walk lay where he was. He didn't speak. His eyes looked wild and were rolled back in his head.

Brave Eagle knew they had to run away. When the Horse Soldiers left, he could slip back to see who was still alive, save some of the food, or at least, to find his bow and arrow.

He caught Long Walk's hand and urged him up. They bent low as they hurried through the trees. Two Horse Soldiers swept around behind them and cut off their retreat.

The soldiers lifted their guns, but a sergeant rode up and shouted at the cavalrymen.

"Cease fire, damnit, Hotchkins!" the Sergeant bellowed. "Don't you know what that means?"

The men put down their weapons.

"Sorry, Sergeant Kincaid. Just following orders. Sergeant Hill told us to wipe out the bastards."

"You had a cease fire, soldier. You obey the last command given, you know that."

Another trooper broke through the brush. He was the same hatless red-haired man Brave Eagle saw kill his mother. The trooper fired at the two Indian boys before he saw the other cavalrymen.

Brave Eagle watched the trooper fire, heard the sound of the bullet hit flesh and bone. Long Walk pitched forward as the bullet tore into his back and came out his chest, stopping his heart forever.

Brave Eagle ran at the red-haired

trooper, his small hunting knife out. The trooper lifted his rifle again.

"Cease fire, trooper!" Sergeant Kincaid bellowed. He spurred his horse forward, dropped off it, catching Brave Eagle from behind, and slamming him to the ground. The fall knocked the wind out of Brave Eagle, and he gasped for breath as he rolled over on his back.

He didn't know where his knife was. He was more concerned with getting another breath. He gagged, struggled, gasped again and again, before he could get enough air into his lungs to breathe normally.

Sergeant Kincaid sat up and held Brave Eagle by one arm. "Private Tucker, you're on extra duty whenever I see your ass, you understand that? Now all three of you get back to the unit."

The three soldiers turned and rode toward the village. Brave Eagle sat up, gasping for air another two or three minutes before he could breathe normally.

Sergeant Kincaid watched the young Indian boy. "Damnit to hell, kid. I don't know how this got started. We was supposed to take your whole band to the reservation. Somebody shot first, and then all hell broke loose. Sure, I know, you don't understand a word I'm saying. I'm gonna try and save you. At least *one* out of the band."

He stood up, shoved his pistol back in his holster, caught his horse's reins and Brave Eagle's wrist. He made the friend sign, with two small fingers held down by his thumb, and pulled Brave Eagle toward the Indian camp that stank of death.

CHAPTER

NINE

The soldier who tugged Brave Eagle along seemed to be a chief. When he yelled, soldiers jumped to obey him. The soldier and Brave Eagle walked into the village, past where his mother and brother lay dead.

Sergeant Kincaid led the Indian boy around the dead, into the middle of the six tipis. The troopers were pulling them down and setting them on fire. The Sergeant came up to Captain Two-Guns Riley on his horse.

"Sir, I've found only one survivor. Not sure if there are any more."

The Captain looked down at Brave Eagle and snorted. "Skinny damn little bird, ain't he? Hell, too bad we have to haul him all the way back to the fort. He might try to get away and you could. . . ." The officer looked down at Sergeant Kincaid over the back of his horse.

"Sir, are you ordering me to kill this prisoner?" the Sergeant asked.

"No, damnit, Kincaid! You trying to get me in trouble? I'll have your ass for that. He's your responsibility to get back to the fort, and then on to the reservation. Your job, you got that?"

"Yes, Sir."

"Now, make damn sure that all this junk is piled up and burned. I don't want you to leave a thing here other Indian tribes could use. Not a tipi tent cover, not a piece of buffalo robe, not a stick to make a fire with. Burn it all up, every bit of it, including any stock of pemmican and buffalo jerky. Get moving, Sergeant!"

Sergeant Kincaid held the Indian boy's wrist as he supervised the burning of the village. It didn't take long. Once the sergeant let go of the boy, Brave Eagle grabbed a three-foot piece of burned tipi pole and charged after Private Tucker, the redhead who had shot his mother, brother, and friend, Long Walk.

Tucker took a blow on the side and turned around, his six-gun coming up just as Sergeant Kincaid got there. Kincaid knocked the club out of the boy's hand and dragged him away.

"Young chief, you trying to get yourself killed? That Tucker is a bad one. He wants to kill you. In fact, he's made a bet that he'll kill you before we get back to the fort. Don't make it easy for him."

Kincaid looked at the young Indian boy and swore. "Damnit, boy, you don't even know what I'm saying."

He tried sign language of his own making. He pointed to Tucker, then to the boy, and made a slashing motion across his throat. He did it twice. The Indian boy pointed to himself, then to Tucker, and made a stabbing sign into the heart.

"Yeah, I get the idea, Chief. You do that and it'll get you killed damn quick."

Two hours later the Comanche camp had been totally destroyed. They shot the Indian ponies. Sergeant Kincaid had saved one for the Comanche boy. He tied the mount to his saddle on a lead line, and they began the march back to the fort.

Twice Brave Eagle untied the lead line and rode away. Each time the sergeant caught him with his big army mount.

"Kid, I picked the scrawniest pony I could find so I could outrun him. Now don't try to get away again, just won't work."

They rode all day and Brave Eagle tried to figure out a way to escape. With a head start, they would never find him. He still knew the country. By the time they stopped for the night he had discovered no way to slip away from the soldier with three yellow stripes on his sleeve.

He ordered around the other men. Two chiefs higher than the three-stripe ordered him around. Brave Eagle did not understand the Horse Soldier's ways. He was impressed with the chiefs' control. The men did as they were told, quickly. Not at all like Indian warriors who followed the war leader, only if they wanted to.

The troop stopped about four o'clock that afternoon. They were another day's ride from their fort. Brave Eagle knew he could slip away in the darkness. The white-eyes would never find him.

That night he was taken to the big chief, who asked him a question. But Brave Eagle did not understand.

"Slimy little heathen, I should just let you have an accident, but I can't. Not with a chance for that promotion. Hell, guess I'll have to use my scout." He called someone who came out of the darkness to the campfire.

Brave Eagle stiffened. A Kiowa, he could tell by the single feather in his hair, and the way he braided his hair!

The Kiowa asked Brave Eagle where the rest of the band could be found. There was a report of 30 tipis in this band, but they had found only six.

Brave Eagle pretended he didn't understand. Quickly the knife of the Kiowa was against Brave Eagle's throat, denting the flesh.

"Tell me, young one, or I'll slit your throat. The Captain here wants me to, so your blood won't be on his hands. Tell me anything or I'll have to kill you."

Brave Eagle trembled. "Twenty warriors and their families went back to join another tribe headed by Young Fox, three days long ride north," Brave Eagle said. He had made up the whole thing. But the pressure on his throat relaxed, and the knife came away.

The hated Kiowa told the Horse Soldier Captain what Brave Eagle had said. It satisfied the big chief. He made a motion with his hand and the Sergeant took Brave Eagle back to their small fire.

The Kiowa was waiting for them, wearing army pants and shirt. He was holding an army carbine. The Sergeant asked the Kiowa many questions to ask of Brave Eagle. He answered them quickly so the Kiowa would not kill him.

He told them that the Horse Soldiers had killed his mother, father, brother, and sister. Short Spear had fired the first shot. Then everyone began shooting at the tipis. The soldiers seemed to enjoy killing the Comanche.

At last, the three-stripe was satisfied and the Kiowa went away. The Sergeant shared his food with Brave Eagle. He said many words. He bound Brave Eagle hand and foot, and then tied one arm to his own. Any movement would waken the white-eye Horse Soldier.

Brave Eagle did not sleep that night as he tried to loosen his bonds without rousing the three-stripes. He could not do it, and toward morning he felt a tear slide down his cheek.

The next morning Brave Eagle sat up sharply, and the three-stripe came up beside him. It was almost dawn. There wouldn't be a cloud in the sky. The Texas weather would be hot and dry. Brave Eagle knew if he didn't get away soon, he would be too far from any Comanches to find his way back.

The white-eye kept talking, but Brave Eagle didn't understand. A few signs that they were developing between them helped. He untied their bonds.

Another three-stripe came and stared hard at Brave Eagle.

"This the runt you saved back at the camp, Kincaid? You always was taking in stray dogs. Wanta make a bet? Just you and me, ride out half a mile with him. Turn him loose and see who can knock the little Comanche bastard off his Indian Pony first. If I do it, you owe me ten bucks. If you hit him first, I owe you. We take turns."

Sergeant Kincaid lunged at Hill but missed him. He stood there glaring at the other noncom.

Sergeant Hill snorted. "Now there you go again, Kincaid, letting that soft streak of yours get in the way. Who's gonna miss one more little savage kid? He's a hostile. No reason to bring him back to camp."

"Did Captain Riley put you up to this, Hill?"

The old Sergeant grinned. "Now that's for me to know, ain't it? You just hush up about the Captain. You want to take the bet or not?"

"Rather the two of us get off a half mile apart, on foot with Spencers and six-guns, and see if I could blow your damn head off. That answer enough for you? Any harm comes to this lad, by anyone, I'm coming after you with a straight razor. You understand me, Hill, you fucking bastard!"

"Yep, the kid is letting his emotions get in the way of his advancement again. Hell, it'll be ten years before you get another stripe, Kincaid. Now just ease up there, boy. I offered you a bet. You don't want to take it, hell, it ain't no hurt on my backside." Sergeant Hill pushed the Indian boy aside and stalked away.

"Sergeant Hill!" Kincaid brayed. The other soldier stopped and looked back.

"You remember what I said about the health of this young man here," Kincaid said softly. "I think I'd enjoy it if you did try something with the boy."

Sergeant Hill glared at the other non-com, then stalked away.

They rode out a half hour later.

There was not a chance to escape. Brave Eagle tried twice. Once, when they stopped for water he was off the horse, running down the middle of the creek. But the three-stripe came splashing after him.

All the way back the Sergeant talked to him. Brave Eagle let the words roll off his back. He didn't have any idea what the white-eye said.

They arrived at the fort just past midday. Ten minutes later Sergeant Kincaid was in the fort commander's office, talking with the Colonel.

"Yes, sir, he was the only survivor, sir."

Colonel Charleston frowned. "I thought this was a simple escort job, taking a small band back to the reservation."

"Yes, sir. I thought so, too. You'll have to talk to Captain Riley about that, sir."

Colonel Charleston nodded. "You don't have to cover up for him, Sergeant. I've known you both for three years now. I know he's a bloody son of a bitch when he wants to be. What happened?"

"I talked to the boy through our Kiowa interpreter. He said a warrior named Short Spear was angry about the move, took out a rifle, and shot a trooper. We returned fire and then everyone began to fire. When it ended, 24 Comaches were dead, including the boy's parents, a brother, and sister."

"Damn shame. So what can we do with him? We can't send him to the reservation by himself. He'd be eaten alive."

"There's an orphanage in town, sir. They have eight or ten children there at the Catholic church boarding home. I'm sure they would take him in."

"Bring in an interpreter," the Colonel said.

A half hour later they found out the boy's name was Brave Eagle. They renamed him Bob Eagle and told him what they were going to do.

"You'll have food, clothes, and a place to live," Sergeant Kincaid told him. "They'll teach you to speak white-eye talk. You seem to be a bright young man. You'll pick it up quickly."

That afternoon Sergeant Kincaid took Bob Eagle to the sisters, who marveled at his jet black hair and dark eyes. They found some clothes for him and showed him his room. The Kiowa went along and Sergeant Kincaid had another talk with the boy.

He made certain that Bob Eagle knew that he was too far from his Comanche people to find them. If he tried, he would probably starve in the desert. He would be better off here, learning to speak and write English, and trying to forget about his family.

Before Kincaid and the Kiowa left, Brave Eagle grasped the white-eye Horse Soldier's forearm and showed him how to grasp his own arm. It was a friend's greeting and a way of saying goodbye. Sergeant Kincaid understood.

Brave Eagle looked at his new home. It was a building made of mud and logs. It was higher than the top of a tipi, with some people living on top of the heads of other people. He sighed. He would stay and learn. One day he would break free and find those Horse Soldiers who had killed his whole family. He beat back tears. A white-eye woman in the long black dress offered a soft hand to lead him up the steps to his room.

He would stay, but only until he was grown-up enough to run away and return to the Comanche people out there somewhere in the Texas high plateau.

CHAPTER

TEN

Boise, Idaho Territory, was the biggest town they had seen during their journey. About ten thousand people, Eagle estimated, as they rumbled along in the Concord coach through town to the stage depot. They had picked up people on the way in until there were twelve riders, three men on top with the luggage, where they hung on with fingernails and toes.

The six men found their blanket rolls and small carpet bags, bought in Pocatello after they had sold their horses and saddles.

They automatically broke into three pairs. They walked down the street toward the first hotel they found, and they registered individually.

Eagle found the closest livery stable and bought a horse and saddle. He haggled for a while, then paid the man, and rode out. He asked directions to Fort Boise. It was a mile northeast of town on Cottonwood Creek.

Eagle rode within sight of the fort, sat under some trees by the creek, and watched the place. There was no fence. The Fort was simply a collection of buildings around a parade ground and a flag pole. He wondered how many troopers were there. Two hundred, maybe as many as 400. It didn't matter. He wasn't going to battle everyone in the fort — just Troop A of the Fourteenth.

Back in town he found Willy Boy. Eagle asked him to pay a call on the fort to find out where Troop A was quartered, and if Captain Riley was still troop commander and Sergeant Kincaid was still with the troop.

Willy put down his cards in a dime-limit poker game. He finished his beer, then went outside. Eagle had been to the barber and his hair was white-eye short. His clothes were strictly cowboy western, and he was trying his best to pass as a white man.

He told Willy Boy what he wanted. It was about three in the afternoon. Willy Boy took Eagle's horse, adjusted the stirrups upward so he could reach them, and rode out to the fort.

Willy Boy went past the guard and the Officer of the Day. At last he talked to the assistant adjutant. His name was Barney Jones, a second lieutenant.

"Troop A, Fourteenth? Sure it's stationed here. What's your interest in that particular troop?"

"I've been hunting my father," Willy Boy said, using his youthful appearance to the hilt. "Someone said he had joined the army again and was with the Fourteenth."

"You said his name was Wilson, Sergeant Wilson?" The man scanned a roster and shook his head. "No Sergeant Wilson in Troop A. They've got a Sergeant Hill and Masters. Captain Riley is the troop commander."

"My dad said something about a Sergeant Kincaid. He still with them?"

"No, that I know for sure. He was killed in an engagement with some Nez Percé about a year ago. Damn good man. If your daddy was with the troop, he sure isn't now. Sorry."

"Maybe if I talked with Sergeant Hill he would remember my father. Would that be possible?"

"Hell, don't see what it would hurt. They're just coming off patrol. Got in about an hour ago. You wait here and I'll have Hill come talk to you. Doubt if it'll do any good. Troopers come in and out of our company all the time. Enlistment runs out, or they just desert."

Willy Boy waited on a bench outside the commander's office. A half hour later Sergeant Hill and another soldier approached him.

"Hear you're looking for your daddy. What was his name again?"

"Wilson, Harry Wilson. I thought he was a sergeant, but maybe he just told me that."

Hill was a large man. His head jutted directly from his shoulders with no discernable neck. His eyes were small, his head big. Rough cut hair framed his face. He was clean-shaven, making his head look larger.

"Wilson . . . Wilson. We had a Wilson about two years ago, a private. Hell, he got shot though. Said he was unmarried. Hell, he wasn't over 18, maybe 19. Couldn't have been him."

"Pa was a redhead. I didn't get any of his hair color."

"Redhead. Nope. I'd remember him for sure. Redheads always give me trouble. Got one in the troop now. Name's Tucker, but he ain't old enough to be your pappy either. You must have the wrong outfit."

"Okay, I'll try somewhere else." He

paused. "Your men live in these buildings?"

"Sure, we're not in tents all the time. Gets cold up here. We're in the second barracks over, the ground floor and the second floor. Army put up some real buildings for a change."

Willy Boy swung up on his horse. He glared right back at the army man. "Hill, I do have one more suggestion. Go to hell!" Willy Boy swung the horse around and rode out of camp.

A half hour later he told Eagle what he had learned about the camp.

"Sergeant Kincaid was killed in a fight with some Nez Percé about a year ago. Sergeant Hill is still with the company. Captain Two-Guns Riley is still the troop commander. Still a captain."

Eagle's eyes gleamed. "Yes. I will meet with both of these men before long. And the redhead. Is he still there?"

"Yes, a private called Tucker."

"He will be first," Eagle said, his eyes hooded. He thanked Willy Boy. He went to a general store to buy a six-inch throwing knife, nicely balanced, three sets of rawhide thongs for lacing up high boots, and a packet of sticker matches. They were sulphur matches glued together on the bottom in a round of wax. He also purchased a half-inch rope, 20 feet long. He paid the store clerk in cash.

Outside, Eagle took a long deep breath and stared up at the sky. "Soon now, spirit of my family and the rest of the people of the White Buffalo band," he whispered. "Soon I will avenge your terrible deaths."

At dark, Eagle rode his horse into the brush along Cottonwood Creek on the far side of the fort. Willy Boy had drawn a rough map of the building where Able Troop had its quarters. He left the woods, slipped unseen through the darkness, past the foolish guards, to the side of the big building.

Eagle watched through a window until he located the redhead. Tucker was telling some wild story and drinking something from a small flask he kept hidden.

Eagle faded into a shadow as a pair of soldiers walked past him on the way to the outhouse.

Eagle grinned. The redheaded one would soon feel the urge to do the same. He waited.

An hour later, Private Tucker made a lewd joke Eagle couldn't quite hear and headed for the door to the outhouse. Eagle hurried across the ground like a shadow and was behind the facility before the trooper left the barracks.

As Tucker reached for the door of the outhouse, Eagle hit him on the side of the head with a hand-sized rock. He caught the lean, tall trooper as he fell unconscious.

Eagle smiled grimly. Now he had the strength of ten men. He lifted Tucker on his shoulders and carried him away from the barracks. At one point he had to wait nearly five minutes while a small group of soldiers shouted and pushed each other, finishing the contents of a quart bottle of whiskey.

Eagle picked up the now tied-up redhead, and carried him past the last barracks into the flat land toward the stream.

Once in the cover of the brush, he draped Tucker over his horse and hauled him a half-mile upstream away from the fort. There were no farms or ranches close by, and no settlement lights.

Eagle found the right spot. He threw the half-inch rope over a limb and tied it so it hung four feet from the ground. Then Eagle stripped the soldier, retied his feet together and his arms to his sides using wet rawhide.

Then, he put one loop snugly around the trooper's throat, and another one around his scrotum. He splashed water in Tucker's face to rouse him.

Tucker bellowed in rage when he came to.

"What the hell? What's going on here? Why am I tied up? Where the hell am I?"

Eagle let him see him in the darkness but said nothing. Tucker began screaming.

"You'll lose your voice doing that Private Tucker," Eagle said.

"Who the fuck are you? What's this about? Hell, I'm naked!"

"True, naked as a baby."

Eagle built a small fire in a spot cleared under the end of the rope. The heavy brush surrounding them protected the light from detection, except at close range.

"What the hell? I know you? This some kind of a joke?"

Eagle lunged for the man as he lay on the ground. His knife point stopped short, nicking the skin under the man's throat near the rawhide.

"Stony Mountain, Texas, do you remember that?"

"Stony Mountain? Hell, we was all over Texas. How am I supposed to remember. . . ."

"The Stony Mountain Massacre, where

24 or 25 Comanches in their small camp were slaughtered by Able Troop of the Fourteenth. Now do you remember?"

"Oh, yeah. That one. So what? We were doing our job."

"Your job was to escort this small, peaceful band of Comanches to the reservation."

"How the hell you know that?"

The blade moved, and in one deft movement cut a slice a quarter of an inch deep down the trooper's right cheek.

"Christ that hurts! You shithead! Why you do that?"

"You were there, Tucker. You ran down a woman holding her two-year-old baby. The little boy was as naked as you are right now. You shot him in the heart."

"Yeah, maybe. How the hell you know that?"

"Then you fired at the mother. At last catching up to her on your horse, you shot her in the face. Then you shot her again in the heart."

"Oh my god! That snot-nosed little Comanche. You had to be there to know all this."

"That rawhide thong around your throat is wet. It's been drying now for about ten minutes. You know what rawhide does when it dries?"

"Sure, it shrinks . . . God you wouldn't do that?"

Eagle sliced Tucker's left cheek with his knife, and the trooper bellowed in pain again.

"Christ, what do you want?"

"What do you think, killer, baby murderer? You killed two members of my family. What do you think I want?"

"No, no, you can't do this. My troop will hunt you down and slice you to bits."

"I got the idea your troop doesn't like you very much, Tucker. Nobody will even miss you. How did Sergeant Kincaid die? Tell me."

"Christ, where did you come from. How'd you know Kincaid got blasted?"

"How did he die? Did the bullet come from his back, not from the enemy?"

"Goddamn, you're too smart for your own good, Comanche."

"Call me Brave Eagle. I am your executioner. It will be a slow death — as slow as I can make it and still get away. You and your troop owe me 24 lives. I intend to even up the score. You're first, because I saw you kill my mother and brother."

"By damn, it is you, that little Injun kid. Knew we should have blasted you too, that day. You won't get away with this. They'll catch you."

"Maybe. But by then you won't care. You'll be dead, rotting along the river bank, unfound, unmourned. You're a dead man already, Tucker, you just happen to be still breathing. How is that rawhide around your throat?"

"Doesn't hurt."

"I'll move you closer to the fire so it'll dry faster." Eagle dragged him closer. Tucker did not complain. Eagle used his knife again, cutting long lines down the tops of both of Tucker's thighs. They were a quarter-inch deep and bled at once, making long red streaks down his legs.

"Bastard!" Tucker screamed.

"How many did you kill that day, Tucker?"

"Half of them! Yeah, at least ten!"

"Then you get a thousand slices of your body. A hundred slices for each Comanche death. It's the custom so their spirits will soar to a higher existence."

"Savage."

"Stupid white-eye."

They stared at each other. Then Eagle built up the fire.

"Hey, that's hot!"

"Hot as hell, like the Catholic sisters always talked about, Tucker? I hope so.

They won't even recognize you when you get to hell."

Tucker looked up in pain at the Indian.

"You enjoy this, don't you, bastard!"

"No, I don't. But it must be done to avenge my family and friends. You must suffer. Your troop must suffer. The U.S. Army must understand it can't kill Indians whenever it wants to." Eagle shot Tucker in the right knee. The bullet smashed directly into the knee joint, shattering it. A bellow of pain issued from Tucker before he fainted.

When Tucker came back to consciousness, his legs had been untied and refastened to stakes in the ground. They were spread wide to expose his genitals. He had been moved closer to the fire, straddling it.

He woke up with a start. He sat up, cringing in pain, as he moved his right knee.

"Bastard! Fucking bastard!" He looked at his legs, the fire, and his crotch. "Damned rawhide is tight!"

"Good, it'll get tighter."

"You Comanche are savages, not fit to live in a civilized world," Tucker screamed.

"You white-eyes are civilized when you shoot down 24 human beings? That's being civilized? You slaughter unarmed men, innocent women, and children. That's what you call white-eye civilization? You're not only stupid, Tucker, you're shitfaced dumb as well."

Eagle shot him in the other knee. Tucker fell backwards, bleating in unbelievable pain, wavering in and out of consciousness. Eagle pushed the small fire closer to Tucker's crotch. The white man screeched in pain as he tried to edge away from the heat.

"Stop it! Take off that rawhide. My nuts are crushing. Please take it . . . ," he gasped for breath. Tucker turned his head. The rawhide cinched tighter around his throat.

"Take it off!" he whispered. He sucked in air and fell slowly backwards.

Eagle touched his neck. With his knife, he cut the rawhide around Tucker's throat. He quickly cut the white man's legs loose and moved them away from the fire. He tied them tightly with rawhide.

When Tucker came back to consciousness, he was disoriented. He bellowed in anger and fear. Slowly his eyes cleared and he realized he was hanging upside down by his ankles.

"What the hell?" he croaked.

"Roasting time, Tucker. You ever seen a man toasted this way? You're hanging over the small fire down below. You can barely feel the heat. But soon I'll lower you down until you'll be warm all over.

"Sure, Tucker, all your hair will burn off and that will hurt. But it won't be anything like later on when the blood in your brain starts to boil. Then your skull will explode like a ripe melon dropped on a big rock!"

"No! Christ, I'll do anything you want me to do. Don't do this!"

"Did you kill my mother and my brother back at Stony Mountain in Texas, Private Tucker?"

Tucker looked away from the man.

Eagle put two more sticks onto the fire to maintain the heat. He went to the rope wrapped around the tree trunk, and eased it gently so Tucker slid down six inches toward the fire. He waited, then lowered the man's body another six inches until he was barely two feet over the flames.

Tucker screamed when his hair caught fire. It burned off in a gush of flames. Then he fainted again.

Eagle raised him three feet above the fire, and waited. He threw water in the killer's face to revive him.

"The pain! The damn pain! Just shoot me and get it over with!"

"No, Tucker. You must suffer. Your army leaders must know you suffered for your brutality. They must understand."

Eagle lowered Tucker toward the flames again. This time he stopped and tied off the rope at the two foot level. He added three more small sticks to the fire. He sat 20 feet away on the cool grass and watched. The killer's body turned slowly as the heat rose and touched it.

Tucker screamed for two minutes. Then his voice failed, and a moment later he passed out.

Eagle added three more small sticks to the fire and waited. It took five minutes. Blood began to drip out of Tucker's ears and nose. The blood in his skull was boiling. In another minute Tucker's skull split open with a hollow snap, and it was over.

Eagle made sure the fire was out. Then he mounted his horse and rode upstream three miles. He made a wide circuit back to a main road, where his horse's prints would be lost in the jumble of traffic. Not even a Comanche could track him back to town or identify the prints.

Eagle put his horse in the livery and walked back to the hotel. It wasn't midnight yet. He found his room, lay down, and stared at the ceiling.

"For you Mama," he said softly. "For you Wandering Horse," he said. Then he went to sleep.

CHAPTER
ELEVEN

Deputy Seth Andrews arrived in Boise almost a week before Willy Boy's Gang got there. He spent most of the first day with the Sheriff of Ada county in downtown Boise. He stared at the wanted poster for several minutes after reading it.

"Seems like these men got into the most trouble after they broke out of jail. Two or three of them might have got a year in prison at the most. I guess I don't rightly understand Texas laws. They're a bit different than the laws that we got around here," said Sheriff Donner.

"Fact remains, the Willy Boy Gang killed over 25 men after they broke jail. By rights I should have been the 26th. You ever seen a man head-shot and live, Sheriff?" Seth took off his hat revealing the small bandage that still covered the worst part of the burn. The hair had not begun to grow back from the scorched scalp.

"Glory be! Powder burn?"

"Right. I was the fool who thought Willy Boy was hanging himself. I seen men hung before. I know how their faces look. I swear he was damn near dead. Then he shot me and laughed. He broke out, and he's been killing and robbing ever since. I lost two good friends that night, and two more the next few days. I got to bring that bunch back to face the court, or bring them back tied over their saddles. One way or the other."

"Do what we can," Sheriff Donner said. "I got me only four deputies. Not a bunch, but all we can afford right now. We can tack these wanteds up all over town. . . ."

Seth held up his hand. "Sheriff, that would just warn them away. I want to see if we can find these men. If we can spot them and arrest them one at a time, they won't be much of a problem. When they all get together they're hell-riding full-tilt on a lightning bolt."

"Do what we can, Deputy."

"I've got detailed descriptions on all six of them. The big guy, the Indian, and the short one, Willy Boy himself, should be the easiest to spot. We can work the saloons and the hotels. Chances are they won't travel as a group. They're too easy to spot that way. I'll talk to your men and give

141

them my descriptions of the gang. All of them are deadly, all killers. Warn your men to be extremely cautious."

"Yep. Two of my deputies will be here in about an hour. Why don't you talk to them this morning. Tonight about seven, you can talk to the other two. Get this thing started."

For the next week they watched the hotels and saloons. But they found no one matching the description of any one of the gang members.

"Maybe they aren't coming," Sheriff Donner said. The Sheriff lit a long black cigar that smelled like burning tar.

"They're coming, you can bet on that," Seth argued. "Boise and the Fourteenth. Brave Eagle has too much hate in his heart not to get here. It's just gonna take them a little longer than I figured."

"So why don't you tell the Colonel at Fort Boise so he can have his guard up?" the cigar smoker asked.

Seth took off his hat and felt of his bandage, as was his habit. "No, I don't think so. They would post a notice or give an order, and the whole damn post would know about it. Then the Indian would be scared off and we'd never see them."

Seth put on his hat and walked around

the office. "Hell, let the army look out for itself. They should know how. You said there were 400 men out there? That should be enough to defend themselves. I'm just one, and you have four deputies. I'll give it another week before I even think about going back home."

Sheriff Donner sighed. "There are other duties for my deputies besides helping you."

"I heard about your crime wave last night. A drunk fell through a saloon window, and one of the fancy women shot a customer in the arm. Things are damn rugged around this town."

Sheriff Donner grinned. "That's the way I like it. Soft, easy, and quiet. When your six friends come into town, there are liable to be bodies falling all over the place. That I can do without. See, if an army boy gets killed off the fort grounds and in the county limits, and he ain't on official business, then I got to take over the investigation and do it jointly with the army. It gets damn complicated."

"Tough, Sheriff. I got to explain to 25 widows why I haven't caught the men who killed their husbands." Seth headed for the door. "Don't mean to matter on this way, Sheriff. I'm getting jumpy, I guess, just waiting for them." He shrugged. "Better go out and work the possibilities. Today might be the day."

He waved and went back to the street. It was after eleven. The morning stage had come in from Twin Falls. That was the right direction at least.

Seth stopped first at the Golden West hotel and nodded at the room clerk, J. Ambrose Puckett. Puckett was a small, slender, sneaky man with a moustache and watery eyes. He seldom looked a person in the eye, rather at his forehead. The tic under his left eye jumped regularly as he grinned at Seth.

"Ah, Deputy Andrews. I think I might have some good news for you. Those men you were looking for. I'm not sure but I think I saw two of them. One was small, five-four maybe, and young. The other one was huge, six-four or so. I'm sure they came in off the morning stage."

Seth pushed a two-and-a-half dollar gold coin over the counter to the clerk.

"Are they in their rooms?"

"No, both went out. The long and the short of it, I'd say. Not sure where they went. Didn't think to tell you about them until they left."

"Watch for the others. You have those

144

descriptions. I'll check back."

Seth hurried out the door and paused. What would he do if he just got into town on the stage, or on horseback? It would be a drink and food, and, for these men, probably a woman.

Directly across the street was a saloon. He didn't look at the name of it. He walked quickly through traffic, missing a large pile left by an oxen, and stomped into the saloon. No women. He'd been in here before and the bar keep knew him by sight.

Seth let his eyes become accustomed to the dimness of the place, then looked at the drinkers at the bar. Nobody was tall. He went to the bar, ordered a nickel beer, and sipped it as he checked the tables.

Somebody just went through the door to the alley. There were a dozen men at the tables, some playing cards, some working on an early beer. At the far table a man leaned his wooden chair back against the wall and sipped at a beer.

For a moment, Seth almost choked on his beer. *It was Gunner Johnson!* The big guy who was slow-witted, but not quite. Seth hadn't even thought about what he would do if he found one of the men alone.

Get what he could get now, he decided. He took his beer and meandered toward the back. He stopped at a table to watch some poker playing. He came up to the big man, and before Gunner could reach for his weapon, Seth jammed his Colt into Gunner's side.

"Gunner, don't move, not a twitch, or I kill you right here." He removed Gunner's big six-gun from the leather and prodded him with his own weapon.

"Up now and walk. We're going outside to the alley. You say a word, signal anyone, or give me any cause at all, and I'll blow your guts wide open. The warrant reads dead or alive, remember? You understand me, Gunner?"

The tall man nodded. "Who . . . who are you?"

"You don't recognize me, Gunner? I'm from Oak Park. I'm the deputy Willy Boy thought he killed when I opened his jail cell. Now move!"

They went into the alley without arousing any attention in the saloon. The strip of barren dirt between the buildings was empty. Businesses backed up to the alley on both sides.

"Walk straight ahead, Gunner. We're going to see the Sheriff."

"Willy Boy didn't kill you back in Texas?"

"No, Gunner, just a crease on my skull and a lot of powder burns on my scalp. I'm fit enough to take all six of you back in irons to hang."

"I don't like that," Gunner said. "But then you ain't even caught us all yet. I reckon you didn't see the Professor come out of that saloon behind us."

"Professor?" Seth could almost feel a .45 caliber slug plowing into his back. But he couldn't turn around. "Gunner, you wouldn't try to play a trick on me, would you?"

"Course not, you being the law and all. The Professor was playing cards and I was to watch for anybody who might be cheating against him. Boy, he's gonna be mad at me."

Seth watched Gunner, tried to move him a little more ahead, then he snapped his head around to look behind at the saloon door.

Gunner's big hand hit Seth's gunhand wrist and slammed the weapon right out of his grip. The six-gun flew to the left out of reach as Gunner rammed his knee into Seth's crotch. The lawman went down in a wailing heap. He pulled his knees up to his chest to lessen the agony.

Seth turned and vomited into the dirt of

the alley. He didn't have strength enough to roll away from the green bile fluid.

Gunner ran quickly down the alley, a lumbering efficient sprint. Then he hurried up the street toward the hotel at a fast walk.

He wasn't sure where anyone was. Eagle went to buy a horse, and Willy Boy was hunting a new hat. The Professor said something about getting his tonsils blown out, whatever that meant.

Gunner went up the stairway to their rooms and found Johnny Joe dressing after his bath.

"That Deputy from Oak Park is in town. The one Willy Boy shot in his cell. He ain't dead. He's here and mad. He got his gun on me, but I got away. We got to tell the rest."

Johnny Joe asked a few quick questions to make sure it was the deputy from Oak Park, Texas. Then he calmed Gunner down. "Pick up your gear. Take everything you own. Go down the street and wait in the alley halfway down from the bank. You know the one? Juan is still in his room. I'll warn him and we'll all get down that way. You get your gear, quick."

Johnny Joe stuffed everything he owned back into his carpetbag and then went to find Juan Romero. Five minutes later both of them went down the side stairs so the desk clerk wouldn't see them.

They found Gunner in the alley. "Stay here and be careful," Johnny Joe said. "I'll go find the Professor." He would be playing cards or whoring, one or the two. Since the girls were probably still sleeping it would be cards, he thought.

Johnny Joe found the Professor at the third saloon he checked and told him about the deputy.

"The guy must be good to track us this far," the Professor said. "Figure that he told the local law about us as well. We better get horses and ride out of town. Buy horses at the livery one at a time. I'll get my gear and meet you down there. Then we try to find Willy Boy and Eagle."

When Willy Boy came back from the fort that first day in Boise, he told Eagle everything he knew. The Indian had absorbed it, then rode off. Willy Boy was sure Eagle was going to get to the work he had to do. When he left Eagle he wandered back to the hotel for a nap before trying some serious poker playing.

Johnny Joe called to Willy Boy just before he went into the hotel. They talked a moment at the side of the hotel. Willy

Boy snorted when he heard about the Oak Park Deputy, then he hurried up to his room returning with his gear. He and Johnny Joe went by the back streets to the livery. A half hour later they rode with the others, north on Cottonwood Creek out of town.

"The fort is out this way about a mile or so," Willy Boy said. "I'm sure that's where Eagle was headed."

"We'll try to meet him on his way back to town," Juan said. "If not, I'll wait for him near his room at the hotel."

They made a small camp along the stream in heavy brush and kept watching for Eagle. Chances were he wouldn't be able to do his work until after dark.

When the night had grown dark enough to hide his features, Juan rode back to the hotel and kept a silent vigil. From a spot near the front door, he sat in a chair tilted back against the wall, resting with his hat over his eyes.

Twice he saw men with deputy sheriff badges walk up the street, but they didn't bother him. No light showed in Eagle's room. It was nearly midnight when Juan saw someone coming up the steps. It was Eagle. But there was no chance to call to him.

Juan hurried up the side stairs to the second floor. By the time he got to Eagle's room, the light was off inside. He knocked on the door and waited. The door was locked and a chair was under the handle.

Juan knocked again harder. This time he heard movement inside.

"Yeah?" a voice came through the door.

"It's Juan," he said.

The door opened. It took half a minute to relock the door and push the chair under it. Juan told him what had happened, Eagle threw the few things back into his carpetbag he had taken out.

They heard footsteps in the hallway.

Eagle lifted the window. He motioned Juan out the window. It was a six-foot drop to the boardwalk hanging by his hands. He made it. Eagle dropped his carpetbag, then the Spencer, and Juan caught both.

Someone banged on the door. "Open up, this is the sheriff!" a harsh voice demanded. Eagle went out the window, and dropped down.

They rode double on Juan's horse to the livery where they saddled Eagle's horse and galloped away into the night.

Eagle rode up beside Juan. "Thank you, my friend. They would have shot me in my bed if you hadn't come. I owe you."

They rode on in the pale moonlight to the Cottonwood River to the hidden camp.

They cheered when Eagle and Juan came in. They were much too close to town so they packed up and rode north three miles in darkness until they found another creek. They settled down for the night in a patch of dense underbrush. In the morning they would figure out what to do.

"My work is partly done here," Eagle said. "I have two more men to reason with. I am grateful for your help. Never could I have done this alone."

"Your turn, redskin," the Professor said. "We pay our dues and we get a shot at our heart's desire. That's the way I figure it."

"Shut up and go to sleep," Willy Boy said, and everyone laughed.

CHAPTER

TWELVE

The next morning Eagle scanned the surrounding countryside. He was delighted with how rich and green it was. August, and the land was green, not burned brown by the sun. Rainfall and surging creeks and rivers seemed to keep the whole valley lush.

He could see no activity either from the fort or the city. If the trooper had been missed, he must not have been found. No one would notice his absence until morning muster.

Eagle set his jaw. The man had deserved to die, and die with great pain. Some of Eagle's great pain of six years was washed away. But there were more men to punish.

Now, the deputy from Texas had arrived to complicate matters.

Eagle climbed down from the tree as Romero was starting a fire. He had carried with him the remains of their trail food. They had coffee, some dry beans, and plenty of dried fruit and jerky.

Willy Boy roused and looked at the fire. He had to make some decisions. When the rest of the men were up, Eagle told them there was no danger of anyone charging into their camp right away.

Willy Boy thanked him. "Eagle, seems you have more business to do with the army. You best take care of that little matter first. Can any of us help you?"

"No," he said quickly. "I must do it myself. This is a matter of vengeance, so my departed family and friends can soar into the higher heaven and live in peace for eternity."

The Professor grinned but said nothing.

"Fine, no rush. We come out here so you'll be able to do your business. No rush at all. Now, our next project is that deputy from Texas. Anybody remember his name?"

"Seth something," Johnny Joe said. "Same as one of my uncles, that's why I remember it."

"Fine. Seth the Deputy. I got to admire that man greatly for tracking us here. I don't know how the hell he did it. But for me, I got nothing against the man. What I'm saying is that we don't blow holes in his head. We don't kill him unless it's a matter of him or us. We go around him.

Anyone have any objections?"

Their heads shook in negation.

"Gunner, he say why he wasn't dead?"

"Said your bullet just grazed his head. Lots of blood and powder burns was all."

"Damn lucky hombre, I'd say," Willy Boy mumbled. "I'll have to be more careful in the future. So, we stay out of Seth's way. Means we'll need some supplies so we can camp out here away from town." He looked around. "Johnny Joe, you're the one of us who's the hardest to identify. Guess it's up to you to go into a couple of stores and buy us some camp-type food."

"I'll tell them it's trail food and get enough for a couple of days," Johnny Joe said. "The next time I'll go to another store. Must be six or eight where we can buy food."

Willy Boy handed him a $20 bill. "From the company fund," Willy Boy said.

Eagle put together a selection of the dried fruit. He centered it on his neckerchief, tied the corners together. He slung it on a rawhide thong around his neck, and arranged it under his shirt.

"I might not be back for a day or two," he said. He honed his hunting knife until the steel was sharp enough to cut a blade of grass without bending it. Satisfied, he

Eagle settled comfortably in a crotch of the tree where he could stretch out his legs. The creek unit worked relentlessly forward, then stopped.

He heard three shots, fired quickly. The search unit was almost swallowed by the trees and brush. The second patrol, moving through the open land, turned and rode in the direction of the shots.

Eagle nodded. It was going as scheduled. Now his problem was to find Sergeant Hill. Six years ago he had learned the men's names from the hated Kiowa during their two-day trip back to the fort. He hadn't forgotten.

He grieved for Sergeant Kincaid. He had been a good man, even for a white-eye, and probably had saved Eagle's life. He would talk to Sergeant Hill about his friend's death. But now, all he could do was wait for darkness.

Sergeant Hill galloped from the open country toward the river. Two blue-shirts waved rifles over their heads. They had found the little bastard by damn! If that drunken private was trying to desert again, he'd cut his balls off. What the hell else could the fucker be doing way up here?

Sergeant Hill arrived ahead of his ten-man detail to the spot beside Cottonwood

Creek where the other troopers stood.

"What the hell you fire for?" he bellowed, as he skidded his horse to a stop and dropped off her neatly. A corporal pointed toward a tree. The troopers moved apart and Sergeant Hill could see a naked form hanging by his heels over what had been a small fire. The man's head had exploded.

"Oh, shit!" He walked up to the corpse and bent to look at what was left of the man's face. He was white. Beside him lay a pair of blue army pants, a shirt, boots and a kerchief.

"Is it Tucker?" he asked the corporal.

"Looks like him. There's a letter in his shirt pocket from some girl in Boston. That's where Tucker is from. He's got a purse with $20 and another letter from his mother in Boston in his pants pocket." The corporal looked away.

"Guess we should cut him down," the corporal said. "Never want to see anything like that again."

"No!" Sergeant Hill barked. "Don't touch him, put his clothes back exactly the way they were. All of you men clear out of here, mount up, ride out a 100 yards, and wait for us."

The men grumbled but left. Sergeant

Hill looked at the corporal and scowled. "Livermore, you should know better. The Captain and the scouts will want to look at him and this whole area to see what they can learn. This ain't no fucking suicide. Somebody killed the bastard Tucker. They'll bust their butts to find out who the murderer is.

"You get on your horse and ride like hell back to camp. Tell Captain Two-Guns what we found. He'll damn well bring the Colonel back here pronto. Now move your ass!"

Sergeant Hill squatted beside the body, staring at the slices on the man's flesh. All had bled, which meant they had been made before he died. On a closer look he saw that both Tucker's knees had been gunshot.

"Jesus H. Kee-rist! Somebody had a lot of hatred to pound out. Who in hell could it be?" Several tribes used the head-roasting method, but the Nez Percé, the Snake or the Shoshoni were not among them. Indian did this? Or a white man who wanted it to *look like an Indian?*

Sergeant Hill walked away and lit up a smoke. He waited 50 yards from the body with his horse for the brass to arrive.

"Goddamn, gonna be hell to pay," Sergeant Hill said. At least none of it would splatter on him.

Later that same day, Eagle lay in the brush of Cottonwood Creek as close to the Horse Soldier camp as he dared. He tried to remember his days in the army fort in Texas. The sergeants lived in the same barracks with their men. Yes, he was sure of it. There had been an open room for the men and separate small rooms on each end for the sergeants and corporals.

How could he get to the Sergeant? Waiting for him to go to the outhouse might take two or three days. How could he get him out of his hole?

Just like getting a big jackrabbit to leave his nest . . . you teased him out. Eagle grinned. He took out a small notebook and a stub pencil from his pocket. He wrote the Sergeant's name on one side, and on the other side he printed a note. It said simply:

"I know who killed Tucker and why. Come alone. Meet 100 steps from the northern paddock fence at nine o'clock. Tucker's friend."

He read it through, and smiled again. He pushed the note in his pocket and waited for full darkness.

An hour after darkness, most of the soldiers were in their barracks. Eagle had little trouble slipping from shadow to shadow toward the barracks. He paused to let the guard pace along his post, then crept into the shadows of the big building, and slid toward the door on the near end.

Eagle used a small folding knife to pin the note to the wooden door with the Sergeant's name.

Then he hurried into the shadows again where he could see the door clearly. Ten minutes later someone came by the door, paused and looked at the note.

"Hey Sarge, something here you should see," the private called.

Sergeant Hill responded in undershirt and pants. He pulled the knife out of the door and looked at the paper, as he carried it inside.

Eagle smiled thinly. The plan was made. The rabbit would come out of his nest. A hundred paces into the area north of the paddock put them 300 yards from any guard post or barracks. It would be perfect. There was no way the Sergeant could bring any men with him. Not unless they got there first.

Eagle would be there waiting within ten minutes. The Sergeant had less than an hour.

★ ★ ★

Sergeant Hill slammed around his room at the end of the barracks. He read the note again. Christ, what was he supposed to do now? This wasn't his job. He should give the note to the Captain and let him deal with it. Yeah, best idea.

He headed for the door, but stopped. On the other hand, if he could talk with this frightened trooper and bring in the killer, it would be a boost toward the sergeant major's job. Old Gunboat Prescot retired next month. Yeah, worth the risk. Damn! He would like to be first soldier of the whole damn post. He'd go. But he'd take some surprises.

No damn trooper was going to get a drop on him. He'd have that derringer hideout, a knife in each boot, and his trusty .45 with six rounds all loaded and ready. Hell, who could hurt him? This was probably some antsy-pantsy softy damn recruit who was scared of his own shit. Yeah, that was it. Some wild-ass found out something and wanted to pass it along without anyone knowing who did it. Yeah, it fit.

He got ready and slid out of the barracks at quarter to nine. If he walked normally he'd be at the spot close enough to nine.

163

Who was going to read a pocket watch by moonlight?

Sergeant Hill flexed his heavy muscles as he walked. He was ready for anything. Hell, he'd wrestled a damn Comanche once in a knife fight and killed the bastard. He wasn't afraid of any man in or out of the army.

He followed the paddock around to the north corner. Then he began counting steps toward the north star. He got to 50, stopped and looked around. Damn prairie almost. A pasture, part of the valley near Cottonwood Creek. A few trees, some scattered brush here and there, mostly low grass and weeds. They let the army horses graze out here sometimes.

Sergeant Hill walked another 50 steps. His eyes were alert as he took the last few yards. He saw nothing. At the 100-step mark, he had his six-gun in one hand and the derringer in the other.

He stopped and turned around completely, but in the darkness could see no one.

"Hey, shithead, I'm here. Sergeant Hill. Now what the hell is this all about?"

He spun around again trying to catch someone sneaking up on him, but there was no one.

"If this is a joke, it's gone too damn far already," he spoke into the darkness.

Then there was a soft whispering, as if a blue jay had cut through the soft night air with rigid wings.

The whisper ended as a six-inch blade drove into Sergeant Hill's back, lanced between his ribs, reaching two inches into the trooper's right lung.

The cavalryman grunted, then fell forward on his face in the grass. He tried to bellow in rage, but somehow he couldn't get enough breath to scream. Air was seeping from the hole in his lung into the small space around it.

Eagle jumped up from his cover of branches and strode up to the fallen soldier. He kicked away the pistol and the six-gun.

"Good evening, Sergeant Hill. Welcome to Stony Mountain, Texas and the reunion of the great Comanche massacre. I was positive that you'd want to be included in the festivities."

"Oh, God," Sergeant Hill said, then he passed out.

CHAPTER

THIRTEEN

Sergeant Hill revived. Eagle sat cross legged in front of him, staring at the white man's shattered face.

"What the hell?" The sergeant wheezed. "Don't talk, Hill, you'll live longer. As I was saying, welcome to the reunion of the Stony Mountain Comanche Massacre of June 14, 1863. Surely you remember. You and your men killed 24 Comanche that day, slaughtered them without warning. You tried to make it 25 for 25, but Sergeant Kincaid stopped you. Remember that, Sergeant Hill?"

The trooper looked up, his eyes glazed with pain and hatred.

"Don't remember," he said.

"Of course you do, Hill. Texas, out of Fort Laurel, under Captain Riley. You were supposed to take our band to the reservation. Chief White Buffalo agreed to go. Then the shooting began."

"Oh, yes."

"I didn't die that day. You're going to pay for your sins. You've pushed a lot of people around, Hill. Now you get pushed. That knife in your back won't kill you, just make you hurt like old Billy Hell for as long as possible. Sit up."

"Can't."

"Sit up or die in five seconds."

He struggled to a sitting position. He touched his holster, but found it empty. His other hand touched his belt, but the hideout was gone.

"I took the knives as well, Hill. You're too weak to use them anyway. How many did you kill that day at Stony Mountain?"

"Don't remember."

Eagle took a knife and cut a slice across Hill's forehead. Blood seeped from the cut and ran down into his eyes. The Sergeant screamed. Eagle slammed his hand into Hill's throat, cutting the scream into a gurgle and shattering Hill's voice box. Hill would never speak or scream again.

He fainted again, falling forward on his side.

Eagle made slices down both of Hill's cheeks, and then splashed water from his canteen into Hill's face. The cavalryman blubbered as he came back to consciousness.

His voice gurgled and his eyes looked out in terror.

"How many Comanche did you kill at the Stony Mountain Massacre, Sergeant Hill?"

He blinked, then held up four fingers.

Brave Eagle growled and waved the bloodied knife near the Sergeant's eyes. Eagle walked away and returned five minutes later with his horse. He lifted the heavy soldier into the saddle, and supported him as they left the fort.

The knife was firmly in place in Hill's back. To remove it would allow the man to bleed profusely. His lung would fail and he would die within minutes.

They walked due north toward the mountains.

The Horse Soldiers would cover a lot of territory quickly on a search. He needed a certain range.

He found it in the darkness three hours later, in the foothills. It was a narrow valley, shielded by firs and pines at the bottom and sides, that opened into a pleasant little meadow a quarter of a mile long. He put the trooper down on his side so he could sleep. He picketed his horse and slept himself, sure that his prisoner would not wander off.

When the sun came up, Brave Eagle was

ready. He had stripped off his white-eye shirt and hat. He had put on his headband and felt more like a Comanche.

He had found a place where little grass grew, cut the four stakes, and sharpened them with one of the trooper's knives. He woke up the Sergeant, cut off his clothes, and took off his boots.

Hill croaked and made angry gestures at him.

"Sergeant Hill, this is the time for retribution. You thought you were going to die before your ugly, murderous behavior caught up with you. You're in luck, you get an early appointment with destiny. Your time is now."

Eagle dragged the heavy man by his shoulders to the selected spot. Once there, he pulled the knife out of Hill's back. He quickly covered the wound with a torn piece of blue shirt. Then he pushed the man to the ground on his back.

Eagle drove one of the stakes into the ground at the Sergeant's wrist. Then he tied the wrist to the stake. The prisoner lay face up, staring at the blue cloudless sky.

Five minutes later the Sergeant was spreadeagled on the warming earth, staked down securely. Eagle took out his knife and honed it. Then lifted one of Hill's eyelids up from his eyeball and sliced the protective flesh away. Blood splattered for a moment.

Hill tried to scream, but only a bleat came from the big body. Eagle cut off the other eyelid. Hill stared at the sky. Soon he would be watching the burning sun with no way to shut it out.

Eagle left Hill there and rode back to the edge of the trees near the valley entrance. From the elevation he could see toward the fort.

It was only an hour after sunrise. He could see no search parties out yet. They would work as they had before, combing the land in all directions.

Eagle went to the woodsy section. He cut branches off a low-growing bush and took them back to Hill. He dug the branch stubs into the ground. He walked back a hundred yards and examined the spot. The branches were high enough to conceal the supine form behind them. Eagle nodded.

The Indian rode his horse into the woods, found a tiny stream. He took a drink, then dug out a pool where the horse could drink. She quickly emptied the pool, then looked up at him.

"Patience, horse. There'll be more water there soon." He picketed the animal so she could drink, or graze on the fall grass. He went back to a shady spot near Sergeant Hill. He was struggling against the rawhide thongs, so he was still alive.

Eagle relaxed on the grass another hour, eating some dried fruit, and drinking at the spring. Then he mounted up and rode back to his lookout point on the little knoll three hundred yards away. He tied his horse and settled down.

He could spot no sign of search for the missing Sergeant. They would figure it out soon. Eagle had made his plans. If a search patrol did blunder into his valley and find Sergeant Hill, he had a counter move. He would put six rounds from the Spencer rifle into the Sergeant, then fade into the timber. Let the white-eyes try to find him.

Eagle leaned back and kept a "soft watch" on the countryside in front of him. Any change in the view would alert him at once.

Captain Two-Guns Riley looked at Corporal Ogden and exploded. "What the hell you mean Sergeant Hill is missing? He was here yesterday. I saw him just after chow. Where the hell is he?"

"I don't know sir. I saw him about seven o'clock. He wasn't there when I went to wake him this morning. I talked to the men. One of them said he found a note with Sergeant Hill's name stuck to the barrack's door with a knife. That was last night about seven, seven-thirty. Hill took the note and went back into his room. Last he saw of him."

"What did the note say?" the Captain asked.

"Nobody saw it. I couldn't find it this morning."

"God damnit to hell! What's going on around here? First Tucker murdered, now Hill is missing." The Captain paced around his office. "Sure he wasn't drinking? He gets blasted on cheap whiskey once in a while."

"No sir. He didn't have a bottle out or nothing when I saw him about eight."

"Lots of time after that to get bombed, go out, and get in trouble. I'll put out a missing-person call at formation and see if anybody has seen him. If not, our company is in shit right up to our chins. We eat shit or die, you understand, Ogden? Now get back to the troop and talk to each man. One of them must know something about Hill, or at least what he was going to do last night."

Ogden saluted and scurried out. He

knew the old man would be mad, but not this wild.

Captain Riley paced his office again. He spread the word about the Sergeant's disappearance at roll call. Then he went to see the Colonel. Might as well spread the news quickly so they could have a chance of finding him. Hill was an old timer. He wouldn't get himself into trouble he couldn't get out of. Hill could match any man on the fort with his fists and feet. He could use his six-gun. Hell, what could have happened to him?

Colonel Vuylsteke threw down a roster of men and leveled his steadiest stare at Riley.

"You saying another man from your company just up and vanished, Captain Riley?"

"Yes sir, I'm afraid so. I don't know why. Both he and Tucker been with the troop for a long time — hell, over seven years at least. We was together in Texas before they shifted us up here."

"You didn't find a thing at morning roll call?"

"No sir. None of the officers or noncoms have seen or heard of him since early last night. He wasn't out drinking with his usual bunch of sergeants."

"Where was Tucker's body found?"

"About two miles out along the Cotton-wood."

"All right. Use your company and pick two more. Start another search. No sense going toward town. Work ten-man patrols out as far as you need to go. That should give you enough men to do a 180-degree search from south to north. Get it moving. And Riley."

"Yes sir."

"If these problems are related, if we find another body out there, you better be ready with a damn lot of answers for me. I want to know what's been going on in your troop. That will be all, Captain."

Captain Riley eased out of the Colonel's door and closed it gently. Then he barged through the outer office and blasted into his Able troop orderly room.

A half hour later the troopers led out in the search. He assigned a sector to each troop. He took the middle one eastward toward Cottonwood Creek. Baker Troop had the northern quadrant and Easy Troop worked the southern third of the sector.

Riley rode beside his second Sergeant, replacing Hill. So the Colonel wanted to know what was going on, did he? Hell, so did Captain Riley.

They worked outward, expanding coverage at the pie-shaped area as they got farther from the fort. It was slow going. Every bit of brush, every tree-lined stream, every hill and swale had to be checked out. He didn't want his men more than 20 feet apart. Soon they began making double sweeps as the search area widened.

They found a wounded coyote and killed it, kicked up two stray cows, and flushed out a nest of skunks. One trooper caught a good squirt of the juice and was sent back to the barracks to wash up.

At the three-mile point they stopped. They adjusted the search zones, then moved out again.

Just before noon Eagle had checked Sergeant Hill. He was still alive, moaning. His eyes rolled back in his head to escape the brilliance of the sun. It baked down on him burning his tender skin. His white body had already turned a bright red. Blisters would soon form.

The trooper breathed, but it was shallow.

"Can you hear me, woman and child killer?"

The man's head nodded.

"During your whole army career, I'm sure there were more innocent people killed, besides my family and friends at Stony Mountain. You deserve to suffer longer, but it looks like you won't make it that long."

Eagle rode back to his observation point. The searchers were working across the valley. He figured they would hit the foothills in two hours. A patrol might penetrate this valley and find Hill by three o'clock.

Eagle lay down to rest. He might have a long night's ride. If white-eyes only came into the valley, he would have no trouble losing them. If some of the Indian scouts and trackers came, it would be tougher. But it would soon be dark, and not even an Indian can track at night.

He dozed, then woke.

The searchers were less than half a mile from the valley. He moved to his predetermined firing position 50 yards uphill from the trooper. Now he sat his bay, waiting. They might come into the valley but not move up far enough to find Hill.

They might.

Twenty minutes later he saw the first two troopers ride into the valley. They sat looking at the open area that extended a quarter of a mile up to more brush and trees.

They had started to turn around when

another man joined them. He shouted something at them, and all three turned and rode up the hill toward the brush.

No rush. Nice and slow and easy. Eagle lifted the Spencer and sighted in. He was only 50 yards away. He could blow the wings off a horsefly at this distance.

He sighted in and waited.

The riders came closer. One swept to the far side, another to the near side where the meadow met the trees. The third one rode straight ahead. He was 20 yards from the concealing branches.

Another few strides on the horse, and the man bellowed in surprise. He lifted his pistol and fired three times.

A fourth shot, heavier this time, thundered into the valley. Then a fifth and a sixth. Two of the three Spencer .52 caliber lead slugs rammed through Sergeant Hill's skull. His head slammed from side to side with the impact.

The three troopers heard the shots, saw the blue pall of smoke from the three rounds, and raced toward him. He knocked down the nearest trooper's horse with a head shot. He stopped the second cavalryman with a round into his shoulder. The third man kicked out of his saddle and ran along behind his mount giving Eagle no sure target.

Eagle turned his bay, kicked her in the flanks, and rode north toward the head of a small ridge through the heavy brush and into denser timber. It was a case of putting some distance between himself and the trooper trying to track him. He made it easy for them. He didn't try to hide his trail. He worked deeper and deeper into the mountains, crossing one ridge line after another.

He heard no one in pursuit. If they were there, they hadn't closed the gap. They would come later. By then he would have doubled back, his tracks lost in one of the streams.

Two down, he thought as he rode. Two of the three men most responsible for the deaths of his people. One to go, one big one who would be harder than ever because of the first two.

He settled into riding through the woods. He realized he had left his shirt somewhere, and wore only his boots, pants and headband.

Like old times, he thought. Like the good times — when he was teaching his young war pony to be guided with his knees, thighs, and toes. He had learned to ride off the saddle that year, hanging onto the horse with one foot tucked under the wide surcingle around his horse's back. He shook his head. Too much thinking about the old days would mean he would greet his ancestors before his appointed time. No, that was something the Sisters at the Catholic white-eye school had taught him, not the old men or the Comanche Medicine men.

He sighed, reloading the Spencer as he rode. He kept going for two hours. Then he paused on a small ridge and looked behind him. It was too forested to find anyone, if they were chasing him.

Eagle rode slower, moving northward until dark. Then he rested the horse for a half hour. He let her drink and graze before he turned at right angles to his northern trek, searching for a small stream to hide his tracks. It would take him most of the night to get back to the Willy Boy camp on the stream, north of Boise.

CHAPTER

FOURTEEN

Willy Boy sat up in his blankets in the little camp on the creek northwest of Boise. He looked at the blankets and grunted. There were five beside him in the little clearing around the fire. Last night there had been four.

Eagle was back.

Willy Boy started a new fire from the coals of last night's blaze. The morning was brisk; he warmed his hands over the fire.

Juan Romero soon woke up and started getting breakfast ready. The less men did, Willy Boy decided, the more they ate. Johnny Joe would need to go into town today for more trail food.

An hour later they were all up. They had eaten flap jacks, bacon, fried potatoes, eggs, and seconds on coffee. Johnny was buying them good food. Eagle had told them he had eliminated two of his targets.

"Just one to go. I really want to find

him," he said. "Captain Two-Guns Riley. He'll be wary now, as cautious as a buck who just heard a gunshot. May take a couple of days."

"You come back for some good food, right?" Romero said, and they all laughed. Nobody commented when Eagle had three helpings of breakfast and cleaned up the rest of the fried potatoes.

Eagle readied his gear to ride again. He saddled his horse, smoothing down the saddle blanket. He tightened the strap and checked the stirrups. He looked up to find Willy Boy watching him.

"This one's going to be a tough one," Willy Boy said. "He'll know somebody is coming. He'll be ready. You want some help?"

The Comanche had put on a shirt and hat so he could ride around the town without notice. He shook his head.

"No, it's still personal. I have to do this myself. A Comanche has to release the last of the Comanche spirits so they can soar into the heavens and finally be free." He watched Willy Boy. A thousand feelings swept over him. He had never thought he could trust a white-eye. They had killed his parents, his relatives. They had pushed him into a school. The nuns had yammered at him. The priests threatened him. At least he had learned the white-eye's way of talking and writing.

But these five white-eyes had been the closest thing to a family he had ever known. They had battled the posse and the bounty hunters together. They had risked their lives for each other. They had a bond that could be broken only by death.

Eagle shook his head. "I'm sorry I can't accept your help. That would make it easier. But my path is not an easy one. I must do it myself."

He hesitated before mounting his bay. "If I am not back here in four days, I won't be coming back. I know I can die as easy as the next man. It could happen. I might be a half-second too slow. I might walk into an ambush. Someone might be hidden in a spot I think safe. It could happen. . . ."

Willy Boy shook his head, laughing softly. "Not to you, Eagle. The whole damn fort couldn't kill you. At least not before you finish your sacred mission. Hurry back. We still have to figure out what to do about our Deputy Sheriff Seth from Oak Park, Texas. He must be going crazy in town."

"We'll work on that when I get back," Eagle said. He stepped into the saddle, looking at Willy Boy seriously. "It's all a big game, Willy Boy. This life. A priest taught me that. He said you had to play it as well as you could, with whatever equipment God gave you. He was right about it being a game. If I win, I'll see you again. If I don't, you continue to play the game for me."

Eagle turned and rode off toward the west. Willy Boy figured the Indian would go in that direction and come at the fort from a different angle — one they didn't expect.

"Good luck, Eagle," Willy Boy said softly, then turned back to the Professor. "Come on now, cardshark. You were going to show us how to deal off the bottom."

The Professor grinned and spread out a blanket in a shady spot.

"Hell, dealing off the bottom is easy. What's hard is getting good enough at it so no one will catch you."

The resulting laughter from the five outlaws reached Eagle. He turned and grinned at them, then hurried ahead. He wanted to ride west of Boise and come up to Cottonwood Creek from the south. He figured the army would have no patrols in that direction.

He turned over in his mind how he

would kill the Captain. Where did the man live on the fort? He must have a house, or rooms of his own. Finding out would have been easier if he had saved the hat and uniform from one of the two dead men.

Too late for that. He thought of other moves. Darkness was his best ally. He would find a place to observe the Horse Soldiers carefully. He wondered what action they would take after two deaths. Would they send out more patrols?

No. They had no specific target or suspect. There was no one they could go out to search for. Good.

Shooting at shadows.

The army would hold fast, watch, and wait.

As they watched, he had time to find the Captain.

He rode half the morning, and then settled on the Cottonwood, a quarter of a mile from Fort Boise. He could see nothing out of the ordinary. Troops of cavalry went through their riding drills. Half the men had never seen a horse before they joined the army. They rode that way.

The bugles blew. The men moved around. A supply wagon train came in from the south in Nevada, where the Southern Pacific had a railroad siding.

He watched companies of infantry in close order drill on the parade grounds. He was continually surprised by the *control* that the white-eye officers had over their troops. The officers said ride or run, and the men did. They said stop, and the blue-shirts stopped.

With the Comanche warriors, each man was a law unto himself. No chief told him what to do. No war party leader *ordered* the warriors to attack, to retreat, or to work an ambush, where timing was so important. The ones who wanted to followed the war leader. This made mass or surprise attacks difficult. He remembered that on most raids some of the warriors attacked early, to capture the best horses or the strongest women.

The rest of the day he watched the soldiers moving back and forth. Drilling, training, building one new barracks from lumber hauled in by the wagon load.

As soon as it was dark, Eagle slipped into the fort grounds. He avoided the interior guard, and hid near the back door of one of the enlisted-men barracks.

Eagle grabbed the second man who appeared. From behind, with his forearm around his throat, he dragged him behind the outhouse. He knocked him out with the butt of his six-gun and quickly took off his uniform. Eagle tore up the man's undershirt. He gagged him, tied him hand and foot, and rolled him further behind the outhouse.

He had looked for a man about his height. So the uniform fit well enough. He could wander around the area with a little more freedom.

Eagle had no hat, but most of the men walking around did not wear their wide-brimmed campaign hats. He walked away from the barracks, across the much-used parade grounds to the line of long one story buildings on the far side. He guessed the officers would be quartered there.

A soldier came down the walkway in front of the quarters. He was a private. Eagle summoned his best soldier slang and waved at the trooper.

"Hey, trying to find Captain Riley's quarters. Got a message for him. Where the hell is it?"

The trooper frowned for a moment, then nodded. "Yeah, down near the other end. He's in quarters number six. This is all shavetails out here."

"Thanks." Eagle plodded on down the line of one story buildings. Some were individual structures. He thought about "shavetail," a term for a new second lieutenant. The word had originated when the army shaved the tails of newly broken-in mules to distinguish them from the experienced mules.

The term had quickly come to mean a brand new second lieutenant and then all lieutenants. It was used in a disparaging manner. The term would probably fade away if the army ever stopped using mules.

He found number six and slipped into the shadows beside the single-family structure. What was he to do now? Knock on the door and parley with the man? Not practical. The Captain would be wary if he received a note, after what happened to Sergeant Hill.

Did the Captain have a family? Eagle didn't want to kill a woman and children. They were innocents. It might be an eye for an eye, as the Sisters used to tell him, but he only wanted Captain Two-Guns.

He decided to wait and see what developed. Perhaps he would have to settle for a long range rifle kill. There was no satisfaction that way. Eagle wanted Captain Two-Guns to know why he was dying. Eagle wanted to see the terror in his eyes. The spirits of 24 Comanches demanded it!

While he waited in the shadows, he

planned his revenge on the Captain. He had never seen the *o-kee-pa* ceremony, but he had heard about it. It was the rite of passage and renewal of life festival used by many of the Plains tribes. He knew how to do it. Yes! But he would need a private place. It would take several hours of blood letting and purification to release the spirits.

He heard the front door open, some voices, and then the door slammed. In the slant of light he had seen a man walk out with the twin gold bars of a captain on his shoulder straps. *It was Captain Two-Guns!* The officer walked down the row of "officer country" buildings and came to another similar quarters. He knocked on the door, then went inside.

Three more men passed as Eagle watched from the deep shadows next to the buildings. A few minutes later he looked in through a window. In a haze of smoke, he saw five men playing cards at a small table.

Eagle made sure he was out of sight. He settled down for a long wait. He was good at waiting. He had learned well how to wait when he was eight. His father had made him put a loop of rawhide cord around a gopher hole. He had to wait until the animal stuck his head out before he could jerk the loop and capture him.

Eagle had sat there for three hours and given up. His father had not scolded him. But the next day he was put down beside another gopher hole and told to stay there until he caught the gopher. The second time it took him nearly six hours before the ground heaved up and a blinking small form pushed out its head. He jerked the rawhide and had his prize.

An Indian must know how to wait.

The poker players might drink as they played. Captain Two-Guns would be tired and maybe a little drunk when the game broke up. He would be easier to capture and transport.

As he waited, Eagle refined his plans for the pleasure of Captain Two-Guns. The game broke up after three hours. The men drifted out. Only Captain Riley had come from this direction. Eagle expected Captain Two-Guns to return.

Captain Two-Guns Riley came out of the door shouting goodbye, teetering as he made the turn towards his quarters. His step was unsteady and irregular as he ambled down the walkway 20 feet.

Eagle caught up with him quickly.

"Captain, let me help you get home," he

said. The Captain turned, angry at first, then he waved and growled.

"Sure. Any hand in a storm, right?"

Eagle made sure the officer had no side arm. As he held him up he could feel no weapon. They went past one building, then turned sharply into the shadows next to it. Eagle laid the cold steel of his razor-edged knife against the Captain's throat.

"Captain Riley, you so much as breathe heavy and I slit your throat. Do you understand? Nod if you do."

The Captain nodded slowly.

"You're coming with me, now, or I'll kill you on the spot. Do you understand?"

Again the army man nodded.

The knife threat had sobered up the man considerably. He walked with more control as they went past the officers' quarters, past another line of Quartermaster buildings, and then beyond, into the open country surrounding the fort.

There was no fence, no guard, no roving patrols. No protection.

With his six-gun Eagle pushed the Captain ahead. The officer stumbled and fell twice. Each time Eagle kicked him, and forced him to rise and walk.

"What . . . what is this about?" the Captain asked.

Eagle didn't answer.

"You an officer? You mad at me and want to fight with me? Don't understand."

"You will, Captain Two-Guns. Try to think back to Texas. I knew you there."

The Captain heard him and must have thought about it, but he didn't reply.

They walked north away from the fort for a quarter of a mile. Then Eagle turned east toward Cottonwood Creek. He needed trees.

They were two miles from the fort when he found the spot he wanted among the trees. He stripped off the Captain's shirt, tied his hands and feet, and left him sitting on the grass under the trees.

"What the hell is this all about?" Captain Riley asked, totally sober now, realizing he was in bad trouble.

"Did you think about Texas, about the Sulphur River, and Stony Mountain? Remember those places?"

"Hell no. I've been on a 100 mountains in my time."

"But on how many mountains did you slaughter 24 Comanche and try for 25?"

"My God! So that's what this is all about? Yeah. Sergeant Hill and Private Tucker were both with me on that raid. Damned savages started shooting. Weren't supposed to shoot. Somebody wounded one of my men."

"So you murdered 24 people when one of your men was *wounded?*"

"It wasn't like that. The shooting started. At first I couldn't stop it. You had to experience it."

"I did, damn you! I was there. I was the twelve-year-old kid who didn't get killed."

"Oh, God!"

"Damn right. Now the other side has the advantage, wouldn't you say, killer?"

"This isn't right. I was doing my duty as a United States Army officer."

"You urged your men on to kill everyone. I heard you Two-Guns Riley."

"Little bastard! You're the one who tortured my two men to death. You're a savage!"

"You think trading three lives for 24 is fair, Captain Riley? Can you tell me who else in your troop was with you at Stony Mountain?"

Captain Riley sat up straighter. "You're going to kill me, aren't you?"

"Eventually."

"Goddamn! I can save you the trouble. Give me my six-gun and one round in it. I can't stand your torture. Never could. Pain scares the hell out of me."

Eagle cut two sticks, green ones as wide as his thumb, into pieces a foot long. He stared at the cavalry officer he had seen ordering his men to slaughter his family and relatives at Stony Mountain.

"Good, Riley. Good. I'm glad pain scares you. You'll get much pain before morning. You'll be so frightened that it might just scare you to death!"

Eagle made a small fire so he could see what he was doing. The fire was well screened from the fort so the interior guards would not see it.

He peeled the bark off the green sticks and cut sharp points on each end.

CHAPTER

FIFTEEN

"Why are you sharpening those sticks? So you can jab me with them?" Captain Riley asked.

"In a way. Captain, have you ever heard of the *o-kee-pa* ceremony of the Plains Indians?"

"Hell no, that ceremonial junk never interested me."

"You should have paid attention. Many tribes put their young men through this rite to determine how brave and strong they are. How well they pass this test will figure just how far they advance in the tribe."

"A pain test?" the captain asked.

"Oh, yes, there is pain. More than any white-eye has ever imagined. I never went through the rites. I was too young before you and your men slaughtered my family and relatives at Stony Mountain. So, now you get to play the part for me. I hope you'll be extremely brave, Captain."

"Yeah, uh, just what. . . ." he swallowed. His eyes shifted as he tried to figure out some way to get free. There was none. "What the hell does this involve?"

"You really want to know?"

"Hell, yes!"

"I'll tell you some of it. To start I'll make four cuts through the skin on your back, two on each side by your shoulder blades. You'll be surprised how tough and strong a man's skin is. These cuts will be about three inches long and an inch and a half apart."

"Yeah, I been cut before. It hurts."

"That's just the start of the hurting, Captain Slaughter. After I make the cuts, I push this sharpened stick in one of the cuts, force it along underneath the inch and half of uncut skin, and out the other side."

"You bastard! I thought you said this was a test!"

"It is Captain, it just hasn't started yet. With the green sticks in place on both sides, I'll tie a strong rope around both ends of each stick. I'll tie the ropes together, toss the end over that branch up there, and lift you off the ground."

"Oh God, no!"

"Captain Murder. You mean you're

afraid of a ritual that a fifteen-year-old Indian boy goes through gladly?"

"That's inhuman! You're a goddamned animal! No wonder you people can do that. You're animals!"

"You may be right, Captain. Let's see if you're as good at being an animal as we are."

Eagle pushed Captain Riley onto his stomach. With his knife he cut four slices in the trooper's skin. They bled a little, but soon the blood stopped. Riley screamed with each cut and was soon blubbering.

Eagle forced the pointed sticks into the first cut, and drove it along under the skin pulling it away from the flesh. The point came out the other side cut and he had his first tie point.

Captain Riley passed out as Eagle inserted the second stake. Eagle quickly tied the small rope around both stick ends and pulled upward. The sticks held and the skin held. Good.

He threw the rope over the limb of a gnarled oak tree. He lifted Captain Riley on his shoulders, pulling the rope as tight as possible and wrapping the slack around his right arm.

Gradually he let the Captain ease off his shoulders. With his full weight hanging the

Captain's skin stretched upward six inches but held and his feet dangled a foot off the ground. Eagle inspected the ties and the green sticks. Everything was done properly and holding.

Good enough.

Eagle tied off the rope around the tree trunk. He filled his hat full of water at the stream. The splash of water in Captain Riley's face brought him sputtering back to consciousness.

He screamed in fear and agony at once.

When the soldier's bellowing trailed off, Eagle stared at him. "The Indian boys never let out a single indication that they felt any pain. They never screamed or yelled or cried out. This would show their weakness and count severely against them." Eagle paused and saw Captain Riley glowering at him.

"Did I tell you the rest of the ritual? I don't think so. After the boy was hung like this, then the medicine man would tie to his ankles a 12- to 15-pound buffalo skull, to make the pain more severe. I'm out of buffalo skulls, so I figure we'll skip that part."

"Bastard! You shitty bastard!"

"So far you would have been cut down and sent out to mind the horses until you became a man. You're not passing the test, Captain Killer Riley. But I'm not going to cut you down."

The Captain's head hung down as he endured the pain.

Eagle touched his arm and turned him around. "Captain, you should be able to see the rest of the scenery. You might not see it for long."

The Captain said nothing and Eagle found the man had passed out again. Another hatful of water brought him back to reality.

"Now, that's better, Captain. I blame you the most for the deaths of my family and friends. Sergeant Hill just did what you told him. Private Tucker was a low-down killer, no matter where he might be. But you, you led these men. You directed them, you *ordered them to kill!*"

With his sharp knife Eagle made a quick slash down his cheeks, as the officer turned slowly.

Riley's thundering roar of terror and pain billowed down the valley. Then his glance shot up at the Indian.

"Savage! Inhuman animal! Killer!"

"No!" Eagle screamed. "I'm not a killer. You are the mass killer who slaughtered 24 defenseless women, children, and Comanche warriors. None of them had a chance. I'm only paying back a small amount — executing those murderers I can find. I know there were nearly 50 of you in Able company. I can't find the rest, but I have found you three. You will pay for your sins . . . NOW!"

A half-dozen more times, Eagle taunted the hanging white-eye. He administered more purifying slashes to the Captain's arms, chest, and face. Blood dripped off his body onto the ground below.

Eagle built up the fire. The 20-minute *o-kee-pa* time limit was long passed. But this was more than just a test, it was an execution.

Each time Eagle sliced the white-eye murderer's flesh, he recited the name of one of his Comanche family or friends who died that day. He said the name ten times. From that time forward, he would refrain from voicing the person's name out loud.

By three o'clock that morning the fire burned low, and the white-eye killer Captain was still alive.

Eagle had gone through the name of each person who had been killed so long ago. He stood before the unconscious Captain. Enough. It was finished.

Eagle thrust the sharp point of his knife

through Captain Riley's heart three times. He wiped the blade clean and went to the stream to wash the blood off his arms and torso. He returned to the faint firelight and quickly gathered up his belongings. He stripped off the army pants and put on his own. He made one last check of the Captain. Yes, he had stopped breathing. No pulse at his wrist. Eagle put on his headband to hold his black hair and trotted the two miles to where he had left his horse.

He rode slowly. The last of the key figures in the massacre at Stony Mountain was dead. He felt a great burden lift from his shoulders. He knew in his heart that the spirits of all 24 Comanches were free at last. They would soar into the higher heavens, and live for all eternity in peace and tranquility.

Eagle rode east into the night. He soon left the valley and climbed into the timbered slopes of the great mountain range. He needed a day alone to cleanse himself, to seek out his own true spirit, and to speak with Cousin Moon, Mother Earth and Father Sun.

A day in the mountains where no white-eye had ever set foot would be ideal. He would ride east until morning. He had no desire to watch the army patrol looking for the Captain.

No one would connect these three executions with the Stony Mountain Massacre. It didn't matter. Not now. The debt was paid, the spirits free. He needed only to purify his own spirit before returning to the Willy Boy Gang.

Yes, he would go back. If it hadn't been for them he would have been a soaring spirit himself.

He owed his allegiance to them for at least a year. By then, his debt paid, he could fade away. He would find his own way in this world of white-eyes. If nothing else, he could always be a cowboy. By the time he was twelve he had learned to ride a horse better than any cowboy would learn in a lifetime. Roping would come easily. Yet he had no desire to be a cowboy.

The white-eye's buffalo were slow and stupid creatures, controlled by the men on horseback. They were not free to roam and live as they pleased. What sport or satisfaction could there be in rounding them up and sending them to the great slaughter houses?

No, he didn't want to be a cowboy.

He rode. Tonight he might find his way, he might have a sign from the great spirit.

A name-change experience even. No, he was not purified for that. He rode on, suddenly interested, eager to get back to his roots, some vestige of his old way of life.

Just before five o'clock that morning, he found a large slab of rock in the mountains facing east. Eagle stripped naked. He lay flat on his back on the rock with his head slightly downhill. The blood would rush to his brain, as the medicine man had instructed him so many years ago.

The weather was brisk. He shivered for a moment, then drawing upon his Comanche blood, he steeled himself. His eyes closed, he let the spirits from the upper heavens bombard him with whatever they wished to communicate.

If anything.

He lay there, felt his head pounding with blood. After an hour he opened his eyes. The sun was just beginning to streak on the horizon. It banished the darkness as it peeked over the jagged hills.

Another hour and the sun's rays crept up to the spot where he still lay.

No spirits had communicated with him. There had been no revelation, no direction.

Had he lost the talent to communicate? Had he been so white-eyed poisoned these last six years that he had lost all ability to contact the great spirit?

If his cousin the Moon could not send him any messages, perhaps his father the Sun could. He would try again. He lay in the bright, harsh, mountain sunshine until midday. The sun was directly overhead.

He felt warm and rested. But again he had received no messages from the spirit world.

Slowly he dressed in the white-eye clothes, laced up his boots, and mounted the white-eye horse. He rode slowly west to the valley. He would skirt around to the north until he could ride into the camp on the second river.

His mind was made up. He would not return to his people. The Comanche would not look on him with favor. He had been damaged in the past six years. He was not sure that he could live as a Comanche again. Over the years he had grown accustomed to the white-eye food and inventions.

Indeed he had been poisoned by the white-eye culture.

What now? He would ride with the outlaws. He would search for a way to make a life for himself in the white-eye world. It would be difficult, but he must.

Clearly the Comanche spirits had not wanted to communicate with him. He was no longer a Comanche. Perhaps there would be a way that he could use that ability to benefit his people.

Eagle was determined to think about the possibilities. He rode, feeling more Comanche than ever, welcoming the sounds of the animals, the soaring of a hawk, blessing Mother Earth for her bounty. He must enjoy it while he could.

Soon he would be half white-eye again.

CHAPTER

SIXTEEN

The six of them sat around the evening cooking fire and talked it out. Eagle had come back late that afternoon and now they were at full strength again.

"Right, I checked it," Johnny Joe said. "Last time I was in Boise I asked about that Deputy Sheriff. Half the town knows him by now. Knows why he's here and all. Seth is staying at the Boise Hotel, third floor on the corner. He eats his meals at the Delmonico café, and spends most of his time talking to the Sheriff."

Willy Boy nodded, his eyes gleaming. "Way I figure it, Deputy Seth is our good luck charm. He got us out of jail. He saved us from being hanged or worse. He's been after us and all has gone well. Don't like to break a string of good luck. We're not going to kill the Deputy."

"Could have a talk with him," the Professor said. "Say we catch him some night without hurting him any, tell him we don't hold no grudge against him for locking us up. Then we take all his clothes off and turn him lose in the middle of Main Street at high noon!"

"Don't like making fun of someone," Gunner said.

"I like it," Romero said. "He's the one who arrested me. He pushed me around like I was filth. I think it's a good thing to show him we can catch him and let him go. That'll make him so mad he won't be able to shoot straight."

Johnny Joe grinned. "Let's try it. Only catch him during the day. Be harder. Anybody can catch a lone man at night in a town. Then we won't have to keep him somewhere until noon the next day. Be simpler."

Eagle laughed softly. "Yes, we catch him. But we better be ready to move out right after we let him go. He'll get a posse roused up fast if he's on such good terms with the local Sheriff. He might even have put together a bounty hunter group by now, just waiting for us to come into town."

Willy Boy threw some more wood on the fire and watched it blaze up. "Always surprises me how things burn up. First it's a solid chunk of wood, and then it burns, goes up in smoke, and it's gone. Destroyed."

The Professor shook his head. "You can't destroy matter, Willy Boy. That piece of wood simply got changed in form. The solid wood changed into smoke, heat, and ash. The matter that was in that piece of wood is still around, just in a different form."

Willy Boy looked up. "You shucking me, Professor?"

"Not at all. Simple, elementary physics. They call it the conservation of matter, as I recall. Matter can't be destroyed, just changed in form. When a piece of wood burns some of it is released in heat — that's energy, some smoke, ash, and gases."

"Be damned," Johnny Joe said. "I thought I was destroying that woodpile."

They laughed. They looked at Willy Boy. He always called the shots for the gang.

"I agree with the majority. I think we should grab the Deputy, have a good talk with him. Tell him to go back home before he gets hurt, then strip him down, and foist him into the middle of Main Street. But I been thinking. He'll just run into a store somewhere.

"How about we padlock a chain to his ankle, and padlock the other end of the chain to a porch roof post?"

They all laughed again, all but Gunner.

"I'll buy the chain and locks tomorrow," Johnny Joe said. "When do we grab him?"

"At noon, right after he finishes eating at that café," Willy Boy said. "First though we need to get our packs ready, our traveling food, and be ready to hit the trail."

"Won't take all six of us to play our trick on the Deputy," Johnny said. "How we going to work it?"

"How far is the café from an alley?" the Professor asked quietly.

"About three doors, as I remember," Johnny Joe said.

"So we grab him at the front door, and hustle him into the alley. We six can have a chat with him there out of sight," the Professor went on. "When our talking is over, we put a gag in his mouth, strip off his clothes, padlock on the chain, and put one of our trail coats on him. Two of us walk him to the post, chain him there, whip off the coat, and run like hell!"

They all laughed.

"Any chances for trouble?" Willy Boy asked.

"Only if the Sheriff or a deputy sees us hustle him into the alley," Eagle said. "Some citizen might think it's a robbery or such."

"So the four of us not making the grab

stay in the alley to cover the two on the street," Willy Boy said. "Same for planting Seth around that porch post." Willy Boy looked at them. "Got to be the Professor and Johnny Joe. Least recognizable of our gang."

Willy Boy looked at Romero. "We'll need food for three days. We'll get more grub when we hit Twin Falls. We'll be heading back down the way we came, all the way to the railroad. Horseback this time, be a sight safer."

"I'm in no rush," Eagle said.

"When we hit the railroad we'll decide which direction to go. We'll all be tired enough riding by then."

Willy Boy watched the men. He knew them better now. Understood their moods and their motives. They all were wondering which direction they would go. He had made up his mind. They were closer to the coast than to Denver. So they would grab the train and ride the rails all the way to San Francisco.

Then they would see how Johnny Joe could do against the best gamblers in the land.

Four of the Willy Boy Gang rode into town about noon the next day. The Professor and Johnny Joe had left earlier to buy the food and get it packed on their two horses. Then they would officiate at the grabbing of Deputy Sheriff Seth near the Delmonico's Cafe.

Willy Boy expected no trouble. Noon was a slow time for most law enforcement people, and the town's real Deputies would be having something to eat or cleaning their weapons.

The four men rode in from two different directions and met in the alley just down from Delmonico's. They tied their horses and moved to the head of the alley to wait.

About twelve-thirty a man came out of the restaurant. The men tensed, but the Professor and Johnny Joe, who now leaned against the building next to the eatery, did not move.

Another 15 minutes went by before Willy Boy saw the Professor and Johnny Joe ease away from the building, and fall into step on each side of an average-sized gent about 35 years old and a little thick at the waist.

Johnny Joe pushed a hand-sized der-ringer into the Deputy's side and held his arm.

"Deputy Sheriff Seth from down in Oak Park, Texas?" Johnny Joe said. "We need a word with you about them outlaws that you're hunting."

"What? Oh, yes. There's no need for the weapon. Have you seen the men, any of the six?"

"We most certainly have, Seth," the Professor said. "Fact is I saw all six of them just this morning."

Seth looked at him sharply. "Oh, Christ, the Professor!"

"Right, and you try to yell and you're dead meat, you know that don't you, Deputy?"

"Yes. I've seen your murderous work before. Where are you taking me? Why not just kill me here?"

They were at the alley by then, sauntered into the opening, and were, at once, gulped down in the shadows.

The Professor cleaned Seth's holster, took a hideout from the belt in the middle of his back and two throwing knives from each boot.

Half way down the alley there was a small offset in a shorter building. They walked into the alcove, out of sight of anyone in the alley.

"You murdering bastards!" Seth, looking around. "You're all here, all six of you. I don't believe it. It's going to take six of you to kill me?"

Willy Boy laughed. "Seth, calm down, nobody is going to kill you. I had my chance in the jail cell, remember. I missed. Far as we're concerned, you're our good luck charm. Everytime you show up something good happens to us. Why would we kill you?"

"You shot down two of my good friends, killed four other men I knew," Seth shouted. "Why?"

Willy Boy's face hardened, a tic grew under his left eye. "Seth you know damned well why. Three of us were up to be hanged, and two others were convicted with little or no evidence. Gunner was innocent of any wrong doing. So Texas law was out to get us. For posse and bounty hunters it works this way: you try to kill me, I've got a right to try to kill you. Don't fuss about those posse members. They knew what they were in for."

"Your gang has killed 25 men since you got out."

"Most of them asked for it. We don't consider bounty hunters as good as lawmen, they're scum." Then Willy Boy brightened. "Hey, this is no time to get mad. Wanted to know how you figured out where we went. It's a big country."

"I talked to them at Fort Dodge. They

said one of you asked about the Four-teenth Cavalry in Boise. I figured you'd be coming here. Easy."

"You're a smart man, Deputy. What's your last name?"

"Andrews."

"Like I was saying, you're a smart man. You've more than done your duty to the folks in Oak Park. You tried harder than any man I ever saw. Now it's time for you give up the chase, get on the stage, and ride back to Texas. You fought a good fight, but it's over now."

"Not by a damn sight! I swore an oath on the bodies of my friends to kill you all or bring you back to trial."

Willy Boy frowned, and lifted his six-gun in and out of the holster. "Deputy Andrews, that kind of talk could get a lawman killed in the blink of an eye. That's stupid talk, emotional. Think it over cold and cool. If you come at us again, we'll kill you for sure. You have any doubts about that?"

Deputy Andrews stared at Willy Boy without flinching. "Not a damn doubt, Willy Boy Lambier. But I got to try."

Willy Boy shrugged. "Hell, we warned you. Maybe between now and the next time, you'll get a good dose of common sense." He looked at Johnny Joe. "Let's do it, boys. Everything else all set?"

"Sure as hell is," Johnny Joe said. He went down the alley 20 feet. He kicked a cardboard box off. It covered a 40-pound square chunk of iron attached by a padlock to a quarter-inch link chain.

He lifted the iron anchor carefully, and carried it to the rest of them. The Professor stripped the Deputy's clothes off over his protests.

"Your clothes and piece will be here when you can come and get them," Willy Boy said. When Andrews was naked, Willy Boy gave him his long heavy coat to hold around his shoulders.

"What the hell you guys doing?" Deputy Andrews bleated.

"See soon enough," Willy Boy said.

The Professor fastened the chain around Andrews' leg and locked it with the padlock.

Gunner stepped up and pointed to the iron. "I'll carry it," he said. The Professor grabbed Deputy Andrews from behind, and Gunner picked up the heavy iron weight. They walked out to the street to the first post supporting the overhang above the boardwalk. Gunner wrapped the weighted end of the chain around the post and put the block of iron beside the post.

Then he slipped a padlock through two links, locking the weight securely in place.

The Professor whipped off the long coat that covered Andrews, leaving him naked. Then he and Gunner sprinted for the alley they had just left. Hoots and catcalls shrilled across the quiet street.

Two women looked at Andrews, then turned their faces away, but they were laughing. The whores in the windows on the other side yelled at Andrews, ridiculing his shriveled-up male member.

The gang's horses had been brought up when Andrews was carried out. Now all six men sat on their mounts and watched the fun.

Two small girls stood and stared as Andrews tried to cover his crotch with his hands. The girls' mother rushed out of the store, laughed at Andrews, and pulled her girls away, down the street.

It was nearly five minutes before a man with a star on his chest ran up. He looked at the locks, then at the post, and hurried down to the blacksmith for a big cold chisel and a heavy hammer.

"Let's go on a ride," Willy Boy said.

The six members of the gang walked their horses in pairs down past Deputy Seth Andrews from Oak Park, Texas, and out of town to the west. As soon as they were a mile from Boise, they swung south and then east to find the stage road that would take them to Twin Falls. It was a little out of their way, but a stage road was easier than trying to grind through the Rocky Mountains without a trail.

"Railroad here we come!" the Professor shouted, when they hit the stage trail.

"Yeah, by damn!" Willy Boy said, and they galloped down the road for a quarter of a mile, just to celebrate.

CHAPTER
SEVENTEEN

On Main Street in Boise, Seth Andrews cowered a few minutes, covering his naked genitals. He had his back turned when the outlaws rode by. He saw them, but there was nothing he could do, yet.

Quickly he shouted at a man on the boardwalk to lend him his plaid shirt. The man stripped it off and Seth wrapped it around his waist, covering his crotch.

He shouted for another deputy who came running.

"Remember that posse we had put together?" Seth said. "I just found the outlaws I'm hunting. Get that posse together in ten minutes, so we can ride."

The Deputy looked at him a minute. "They do this to you, the desperate outlaws you're tracking down?"

"Yes, it's harassment. Now move!"

The first Deputy came back with a cold chisel and a five-pound hammer, and a blacksmith to swing it. He whopped the chain apart near the post with ten solid blows of the big hammer. Then he had Seth move close to the chunk of iron. The blacksmith worked on the links around his leg. He couldn't get the link in a position to strike without hurting Seth's leg.

The hardware store owner ran up with a box full of padlocks. He looked at the one on the chain. He selected a box of the same make lock, and opened it. The keys to that lock wouldn't work. He tried another box, again no luck.

Then he took two small pieces of steel wire. He pushed them into the padlock, turned and pushed again, and a moment later the lock came open.

Seth ran to the alley, found his clothes, and dressed. Even his six-gun was still there, his hideout and his knives. He replaced everything and rushed down to the Sheriff's office.

"Of course they rode out to the west, that means they're going to head back east. He's from Missouri," Seth argued.

At last they split their posse in two sections, five men each. Seth led his five men out to the east down the stage road to Twin Falls.

He had a rifle in his boot and 30 rounds.

He just hoped they got close enough to use it.

Seth felt the incident caused more professional chagrin than personal embarrassment. He'd been naked before. What hurt was the way they so easily captured him, stripped him, and let him go without a cut or a scratch. They had even been polite! They could have tortured and murdered him.

That alone made him even more furious. How could he go home, and report that he had contacted them and they got away? He couldn't go home until they were dead. Seth Andrews set his jaw and rode faster down the stage road.

Three miles out of town they cut a trail of six or seven horses coming in from the west. Yes! Had them by god! It had taken almost an hour to get the posse moving. But with the long loop the outlaws had made to the west, they couldn't be more than a half hour ahead of him now.

Seth pushed his five men harder. They topped a small rise and looked ahead. No sign of six riders.

He rode faster until he realized he was going to use up his mounts at this speed, and they all would soon be on foot. Grudgingly he slowed to a walk and let the horses catch their wind.

The bastards! How could they do that to him? Why not just write him a note and then leave town? No, they had to wound his pride and destroy what little credence he had in Boise. They would pay. By damn, everyone of them would pay!

A mile farther on he stopped and checked the trail. He could still see the six set of prints moving southeast. They didn't seem to be riding fast. He should catch them before dark.

But two hours later, he seemed no closer to them. The little posse had settled down to an easy six-miles-an-hour canter, that was easy on the horses but harder on the men.

"We've got to find them before dark, or it could be trouble," Seth Andrews told his five men.

In a patch of brush and hard wood near a small stream, Willy Boy and his gang sat on their horses, and watched Seth and his five men ride by on the stage trail two hundred yards away. Each of the outlaws held his horse's muzzle, so she could not "horse talk" to the other animals.

When the posse was past, Eagle rode down the creek to watch the men and see if they kept going.

"Is that it?" Gunner asked. "Are they gone?"

"For a minute. I'd bet that Seth is checking the prints every mile or two, which means they could be doubling back and looking for us again within 15 or 20 minutes."

"Set up an ambush?" the Professor said. "We could cut down the five posse members, and let Seth ride away unscratched."

"We could," Johnny Joe said. "But it really ain't their fight. Why don't we just hightail it through the open spaces and leave some confusing trails. That bunch could never track us."

"We'll let Seth call the tune," Willy Boy said. "Let's set up an ambush. If Eagle comes back and says they're returning, we'll decide what to do."

Five minutes later they were spread in an arc to give them crossfire without endangering themselves. They were off their mounts, behind larger trees or logs with good fields of fire.

It was another five minutes before Eagle rode back fast.

"They're coming back," he said. He saw the spread and picked his own spot. He put his horse with the others, out of danger.

Willy called to the troops. "When they come down the stage road to where we turned off, they'll turn this way. We put two rounds of rifle fire over their heads. Then I'll have a little chat with Seth and send him home."

"What if it don't work?" Romero asked.

"Then we'll try something else. Hell, we can always shoot them down."

The outlaws heard the posse before they saw the men. They came pounding down along the road. Just past a spray of trees, they came in sight and found the spot the outlaws left the road.

They rode off the trail a dozen rods and Seth stopped them. He looked at the woods ahead and must have remembered ambushes. Then he shrugged, gave a command, and the six men galloped full speed for the trees 200 yards away.

"Two over their heads!" Willy Boy shouted.

The six rifles fired twice each. One of the posse members spun around, and rode away as fast as he had been coming forward.

Two more slowed. At last Seth slowed himself and stopped.

"Willy Boy, you shoot better than that at 200 yards," Seth bellowed.

"Damn true, Seth. Get your ass out of there before we blow it away. You don't stand a chance. Neither do those cock-lickers riding with you."

The four remaining men scowled at this, but had come up even with Seth. The Deputy worked his mouth and rubbed his jaw, trying to think it through.

"Ain't got all day, Seth. All five of you are in our sights right now, about a tenth of a second from being dead and laid out. You want that?"

One of the men in the posse turned and galloped away. Seth never glanced at him. "You're a murdering bunch of bastards and I intend to take you in!" Seth screeched, his voice rising in anger.

"Seth, you're not even trying to be nice," Willy Boy said. "Let me put it this way. Now there are four of you out there and six of us in here. Each one of you is sighted in by one rifleman, and two of you have two guns on you. What do you think your chances are?"

Another posse-man turned and galloped back toward town.

"That makes it two to one odds, Seth, and you're in the open and we have cover. Give you any ideas?"

"Damn you!" Seth sputtered, so angry

he could hardly talk.

"Seth, if you want to walk back to town, you sit there another 60 seconds and all three of your horses die. How are you at walking?"

Slowly Seth lifted his hand, turned his mount, and walked carefully back the way they had come. The other two posse members went with him.

"You finally got some smart!" the Professor shouted. Eagle tailed them half way back to town. He caught up with the other five outlaws as they worked along the trail toward Twin Falls.

"They won't be back," Eagle said. "You worked them just right. And without firing a damn shot."

"Hell, I couldn't let any shooting get started. I know what lousy shots you guys are. You'd probably hit Seth by mistake."

They all yelled at Willy Boy, and then laughed.

The three-day ride to Twin Falls gave each man time to think over his position and his future in the Willy Boy Gang.

Juan Romero hadn't changed his mind. He was glad to be alive and free. He would spend a year with the gang, if it held together that long. That was his commitment to the group for getting him out of jail, where he was on a trumped up charge. Then he would go to Mexico to be with his wife Juanita and his year-old son Ernesto. Until then he would send most of his money to Juanita.

The Professor grinned as he rode along. He was free, and playing the joker in this deck. Sooner or later they would get to Denver, and to that bank where they used sawed-off shotguns, and where he almost died. He'd have his crack at that bank with a smooth operating team, professionals who had done it many times before.

Yeah, he had a good thing going here. Six or eight months more, and they should get around to Denver. He expected they would head for San Francisco, since they were closer to the coast than to Denver. On the train, it didn't matter. He reset his hat on his head and grinned. Yeah, it was a good day to *still be alive!*

Eagle rode his horse with the white-eye saddle, his shirt on. He still wore his headband. Out here it didn't matter, and it helped him dream — he was a Comanche warrior heading out on a raid against some terrible traditional Indian tribe enemy.

He was relaxed. For the first time in six years he felt at peace. He had struck the enemy; he had made up, in one small way, for that horrendous day at Stony Mountain. Now it was done, he was free of the burden, and he would stay with this group until the others had had their day in the sun. Then he would be released and free to go his own way. A few more months. Then he would have to decide what to do since he was now convinced he was a Man-In-Two-Camps.

Johnny Joe whistled as he rode along the trail to Twin Falls. He wasn't sure, but there was a 50-50 chance they were heading for San Francisco and his showdown with Francis X. Delany. He had been dreaming of this day for almost two years. If they did head that way, they would need some extra cash. Which could mean a bank or two. Maybe he could borrow some bank loot from the other men.

He'd need at least ten thousand, and right now he had about three thousand. Not insurmountable. He was tired of playing the penny ante games on the trail. He hankered for some big stakes poker. San Francisco was the place, the capital of the poker players. If he had the skill and luck to beat Francis X. Delany, he might stay and open his own gaming house. That was the big step. Hell, he'd be ready to die if he could just whip Delany at his own game. Damn yes!

Gunner rode along beside Willy Boy. He had decided that he would ride with the small man wherever he went, try to protect him, to take care of him. He knew Willy Boy could take care of himself with his guns, but if it turned into a fist fight, Willy Boy would go down with the first punch.

So far there hadn't been any need for Gunner's protection. That was good. Maybe because he stood beside or behind the small man, others had backed away. Yes, he figured it must have happened several times. Gunner grinned as he rode. That was what he was planning to do for as long as he could. Stick close to Willy Boy and keep him out of trouble. He'd do it now and for as long as he could . . .

Willy Boy rode at the head of the little band, working down toward Twin Falls. He laughed softly when he remembered the expression on Deputy Seth Andrews' face. He knew he was beaten back there. He had no where to go. He hadn't even taken his six-gun out of leather.

Willy Boy knew he wasn't going soft. A lesser man might have blasted the lawman in the alley and rode away. But Willy Boy had a finer sense of justice than that. The man was a good luck charm. He wanted him alive. It was a kind of protection that he had no other way of finding. Besides, Seth would suffer a hundred times, remembering the humiliation of being stripped and chained to a post, naked in the middle of town.

And he'd have to relive how he backed down in the face of a fight back at the ambush. Both incidents would goad the lawman everyday for the rest of his life.

Willy Boy smiled as they rode on. Watch out San Francisco, here comes Willy Boy and the outlaws!

The employees of Thorndike Press hope you have enjoyed this Large Print book. All our Thorndike and Wheeler Large Print titles are designed for easy reading, and all our books are made to last. Other Thorndike Press Large Print books are available at your library, through selected bookstores, or directly from us.

For information about titles, please call:

(800) 223-1244

or visit our Web site at:

www.gale.com/thorndike
www.gale.com/wheeler

To share your comments, please write:

Publisher
Thorndike Press
295 Kennedy Memorial Drive
Waterville, ME   04901